A Golden Sunbeam

Miriam's Journal

A Fruitful Vine
A Winding Path
A Joyous Heart
A Treasured Friendship
A Golden Sunbeam

Also by Carrie Bender

WHISPERING BROOK SERIES

Whispering Brook Farm
Summerville Days

Carrie Bender

A Golden Sunbeam

HERALD PRESS
Scottdale, Pennsylvania
Waterloo, Ontario

Library of Congress Cataloging-in-Publication Data
Bender, Carrie, date.
    A golden sunbeam / Carrie Bender.
        p. cm. — (Miriam's journal ; 5)
    ISBN 0-8361-9055-6 (alk. paper)
        I. Title. II. Series: Bender, Carrie, date. Miriam's journal : 5.
PS3552.E53845G65 1996
813'.54—dc20   96-25796
                                                                   CIP

The paper in this publication is recycled and meets the minimum re-
quirements of American National Standard for Information Sciences—
Permanence of Paper for Printed Library Materials, ANSI Z39.48-1984.

Except as otherwise noted, Scripture is based on the *King James Version
of the Holy Bible*, with some adaptation to current English usage. For a
list of Scripture references, see the back of the book. For Jan. 15 and
June 10 in year 16, and March 20 in year 20, thoughts are adapted or
quoted from *The Home Beautiful* (1912), by J. R. Miller, reprinted by
Pathway Publishing Co. For June 23, year 14, the story about Henry
Yoder is retold and adapted from *A Wing and a Prayer,* by Paul Hostet-
ler, copyright © 1993 by Evangel Publishing House, and used by permission; and the story about Yonie Kauffman is retold from *Young Com-
panion* magazine and *The Wasted Years,* copyright Pathway Publishing
Co., and used by permission. The Serenity Prayer for Oct. 29, year 13, is
attributed to Reinhold Niebuhr.

A GOLDEN SUNBEAM
Copyright © 1996 by Herald Press, Scottdale, Pa. 15683
        Published simultaneously in Canada by Herald Press,
        Waterloo, Ont. N2L 6H7. All rights reserved
Library of Congress Catalog Number: 96-25796
International Standard Book Number: 0-8361-9055-6
Printed in the United States of America
Cover art and inside line drawings by Joy Dunn Keenan
Book design by Paula Johnson
Series logo by Merrill R. Miller

05 04 03 02 01 00 99 98 97 96 10 9 8 7 6 5 4 3 2 1

*To all who wrote to me
and encouraged me
to keep on writing*

Contents

⊞

The Author

The author's pen name is Carrie Bender. She is a member of an old order group. With her husband and children, she lives among the Amish in Lancaster County, Pennsylvania.

Reconciled

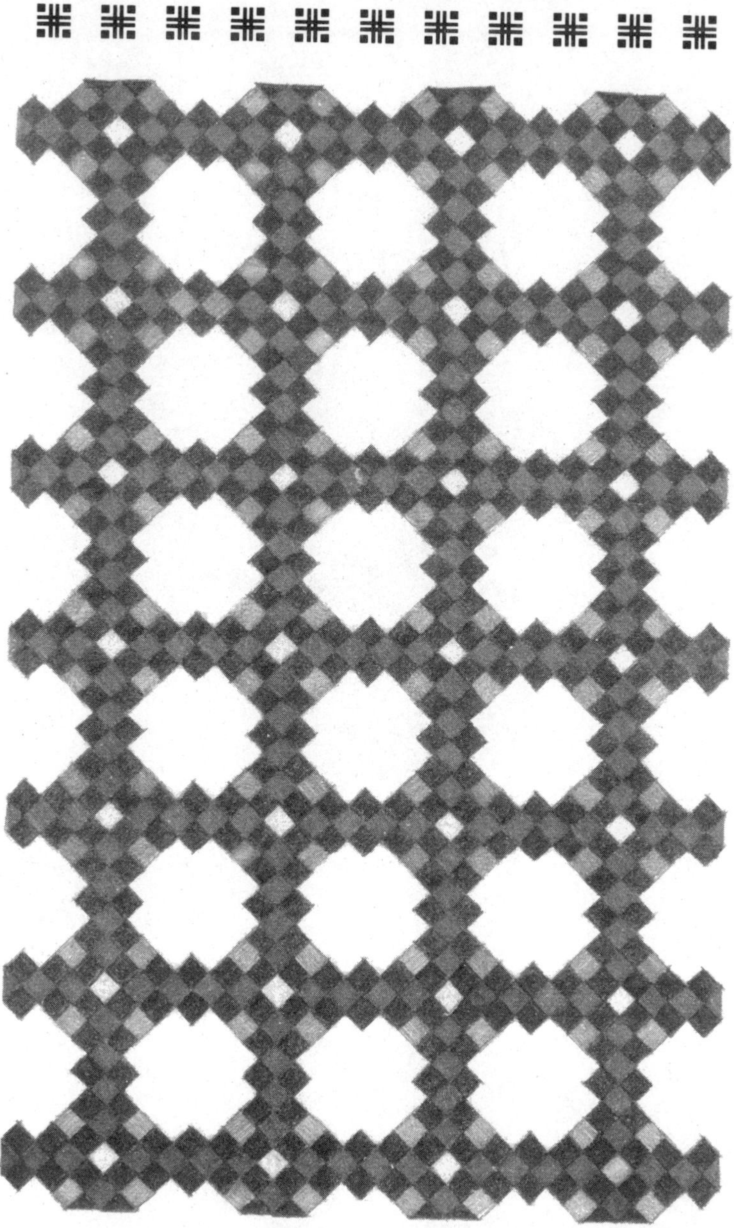

※ ※ ※ ※ ※ ※ ※ ※ ※ ※ ※

July 24

Wwhat is lovelier than strolling down to the meadow on a clear summer's eve? Son Peter and I went to bring up a wayward cow tonight. I was newly awestruck by the majestic beauties of nature all around us.

The grand old trees were silhouetted against the light blue sky with fluffy white clouds floating above them. The loveliness of the woods against the clear sky made quite a picture. The creek water sparkled and sang over the stones while a cool, refreshing breeze softly caressed us. The grandeur of it all put a worshipful feeling of praise to the Creator into my heart.

Peter noticed the beauty too, for he said, "I don't blame the cow for wanting to stay out here instead of going into the barn."

These past few weeks have been such happy ones, filled with days in which we once again felt like working and making plans. It was good to sing and laugh again. Right now we feel as if we'll never again take life and health and each other for granted. Our minds are still so fresh with the memory of how uncertain these things are. We rejoice in our blessings while we have them.

Husband Nate didn't really discover the lump he had under his arm until shortly before he went to the doctor.

Yet just the other day he admitted that ever since last fall, he had a fleeting, unpleasant feeling there now and then. It was like the pain from a dentist lightly touching a nerve while working on a tooth without Novocain, but not as bad.

His suffering was enough to make him feel irritable. I still can hardly believe the results of the biopsy. The lump was benign and not malignant. What a relief!

We found Old Bossy behind a clump of wild rose bushes, and Peter said excitedly, *"Die Kuh is frisch worre!*

(the cow has freshened)."

Indeed, there was a wet, wobbly newborn calf with Old Bossy, and it was cute, looking healthy, and nuzzling for milk. Mama cow mooed protectively, with maybe just a hint of pride in her voice, too.

Yes, those days of fear, dread, and uncertainty now seem like a bad dream: when you wake up, you are so relieved that it was just a dream. Ever present in my mind, though, is the realization that we do not know what the future holds, but we know Who holds the future.

> The clock of life is wound but once,
> And no one has the power
> To tell just when the hands will STOP,
> At late or early hour.
>
> Now is the only time you own.
> Live, love, toil with a will.
> Place no faith in tomorrow.
> The hands may then be still.

—Unknown ▦

August 11

We are in the midst of a shimmering heat wave. The cows stay under shade trees in the meadow or wade belly deep into the creek to cool off. We're hoping for a good, cooling, refreshing rain. The fields of golden rippling grain have been threshed, and next to harvest will be the corn. If it doesn't rain soon, it will mean an extra early start at silo filling.

Henry and Priscilla and their two little girls were here tonight and brought our Dora back at last. Dora had lived as part of our family for years, beginning when Priscilla was desperately ill. But most of this summer she was with her mother and stepfather, Priscilla and Henry, not even coming home for weekends.

Now she had stepped on a rusty nail, barefooted, so they brought her back to visit while it heals. We'll have to soak her foot in Epsom-salt water several times a day to draw out the infection. I'm so glad to have Dora back; I sure missed her a lot.

I can hardly believe how much Dora has matured since spring. Is it possible that our little *Gschenk* (gift) baby is growing up so fast? Ten years old already!

Miriam Joy is such a bright child, ahead of her age, and baby Bathsheba is sweet and cuddly.

However, something lies heavy on my heart. Henry and Priscilla both seemed quiet and preoccupied when they were here. Several times I thought Henry was about to say something, but then at the last instant he changed his mind. It gave me a feeling of foreboding. What could be wrong now? Surely they're not getting weak in the faith again. Let's hope it's not that.

I stood at the window and watched them climb into the carriage and slowly wend their way out the lane. Nate came in and joined me at the window.

"What do you think was bothering them tonight?" I asked him. "It seemed like they had something on their minds."

"That's what wonders me, too," Nate replied. "I know one thing: Henry is getting tired of his carpenter job. He said tonight that he needs a change."

A hazy orange moon was rising above the trees, and it made a beam of sparkling light on the creek. Dora sat on the porch looking wistfully after Henry's carriage. Peter, Sadie, and Crist were romping on the lawn.

"Nate," I said, with a catch in my voice, "I feel . . . , I'm afraid . . . that we're losing Dora. Somehow she doesn't seem like our daughter anymore. Do you feel it, too?"

Nate shook his head. "It's just because she was away all summer," he said comfortingly. "She'll soon seem like one of us again."

"But she seems so different," I said worriedly. "Almost as if someone turned her against us."

"Nonsense," Nate scoffed. "She's just changing because she's growing up. You can't keep her a little girl always, nor tie her to your apron strings."

"But she still *is* a little girl," I protested. "I'm afraid Henry and Priscilla have been so preoccupied that it affected Dora. I know they had something on their minds and didn't have the courage to say it."

"Maybe you're just jumping to conclusions," Nate suggested. "You've done that before, you know, and it didn't mean a thing then."

"But I'm afraid Henry and Priscilla are wanting their daughter back," I blurted out. Finally I had brought my fears into the open.

Nate stared at me for a few moments. Then he said, "Well, you know that Dora was a gift to us and that Priscilla is her real mother. We should be glad that we've had her for as long as we did.

"If they want her back, we'll have to say like we did when Amanda died: 'The Lord has given, and the Lord has

_15_

taken away. Blessed be the name of the Lord.' ''

"Oh, Nate," I cried reproachfully, "how could you take it so calmly? Wouldn't you even care?"

"You know I would!" Nate was quick to reply. "There's always been a special bond between Dora and me, too. But I'm not going to borrow trouble and worry about something that will probably never happen."

The children came running in from their play then, and Sadie got the foot tubs to wash their dusty bare feet. After saying their evening prayers, they scampered happily off to bed.

Dora came in and sat on the settee. I got her some Epsom-salt water to soak her foot in.

"Mom," she said, "do you know that Henry can talk in five different languages? He's teaching Priscilla and me another language, too. Every evening he gives us lessons."

"Whatever for? Isn't German and English enough?"

"It might come in handy someday," was all Dora said. Then she quickly went off to bed, as if she was afraid I'd ask her more.

"*Unvergleichlich!* (strange)," Nate exclaimed. "I guess he knew those languages from his *englisch* days, before he joined the Amish. Or perhaps he's studying books from the library. Maybe they do have something up their sleeves."

He went out to check on another cow that is freshening.

I sat there pondering these things in my heart. It seems that as soon as one thing is settled, something else turns up. Such, I suppose, is life. ❖

We had a heavy thunder-
shower this afternoon with loud claps of thunder and bolts
of lightning. The rain was welcome, but the air is still sul-
try. I don't think it cooled off a bit. I'm looking forward to
the cooler fall weather, when the cornfields will be bare
again.

Pamela Styer came to visit tonight. The kitchen was
warm from canning tomato juice and red beets.

"Whew!" she exclaimed as she sat on the bench and
fanned herself with the *Lancaster Farming* newspaper.
"Sometimes I wonder how you guys survive without air
conditioning. It feels like an oven in here."

I suggested, "Let's sit outside on the porch swing.
There might be a bit of a breeze going there." I gave her
my pleated floral hand fan and took the newspaper as my
fan.

"I have news for you," Pam said happily. "Your German girl is coming in two weeks!"

"Two weeks!" I echoed. "I'll have to get the house
cleaned up before then. And I hope it will be a lot cooler
by that time."

"Don't worry. This girl isn't from a rich family, so she's
not used to the luxuries of life either. She'll be able to
make herself right at home here," Pam assured me.

"How do you know?" I wondered.

"We lived in Germany for two years, and we know the
family, although we weren't close friends. Her name is
Martha Brunner."

"Martha!" I exclaimed. "Why, that's an Amish name."

"Not really," Pam said. "More and more people are going back to good, solid biblical names these days."

"Is she an exchange student? Will she be going to school?"

"Oh no, she's through high school, and she won't be going to college, at least not right away. Her mother died when she was small, and her dad is getting remarried soon. Martha doesn't want to live with her stepmother, so she chose this program. She was a friend of the German girl who lived with an Amish family last year and came back with glowing reports. Martha's really interested in the Amish people."

"Do you mean to say that she's interested in joining the Amish?" I asked.

"Oh no, I'm sure she's not. She just wants to learn more about you people. When she heard how much her friend enjoyed living with an Amish family, she decided that's what she wanted, too."

"Oh dear," I said. "I'm afraid we won't measure up to what she expects. What if she doesn't like it here?"

"She will," Pam assured me.

But I still have my doubts. I'm getting excited about it, though, and eager to see what Martha is like. What if she is another Franie?" ▓

August 31

*T*oday was the first day of school, and little Crist was eager and excited about going to school for the first time. Can it be possible that my baby is a scholar already?

I kept wondering what the new teacher, Melvin Yoder,

is like. I saw him at church on Sunday, and he didn't look at all like what I had imagined. I thought he'd probably be thin and studious looking, wear horn-rimmed glasses, and be stoop-shouldered. But instead he has a round face, curly black hair, and is broad shouldered and muscular.

The teacher is boarding with Rudy and Barbianne, and he rides horseback to school every morning although it's not too far for him to walk.

The house seemed lonely and empty without the children's cheerful voices and the usual squabbling. I escaped to my favorite spot along the creek. It's a place where the water is shallow, and it chatters swiftly and noisily over the rocks, then slips into a deep, quiet, sheltered pool.

That creek is just like a Christian's life—sometimes rough and turbulent, and sometimes tranquil, peaceful, and sheltered. We need to seek a tranquil, quiet spot every day to commune with God, to nourish our souls, to seek the strength that will make us fit for Christian living.

Dora is back with Priscilla and Henry again and going to school from there, so she wasn't along when the children burst into the kitchen at lunchtime.

Eight-year-old Peter happily reported, "Teacher Melvin played baseball with us at recess, and he hit a home run!"

Sadie, seven years old, was enthusiastic and danced around in her school dress and *Schatzli* (little apron). "I asked Teacher Melvin if I may take my doll along to school, and he said yes!"

Little Crist, his eyes sparkling, exclaimed, "Teacher Melvin gave me a new pencil and an eraser and a tablet!"

They seemed happy with their teacher. But I missed Dora and wished I could hear what she had to say about him. Henry and Priscilla with several neighbors had a telephone installed in a shanty so near their house that they can hear it ring. Maybe tonight I'll run out to our neighborhood phone shanty and call them. ▦

*M*artha Brunner is here! Pam brought her this forenoon, and she made herself at home right away! She's not at all shy. Martha has a gift for putting everyone at ease. I believe you'd say she has a bubbly personality; everything seems to amuse and delight her. I wonder if she never gets out of sorts.

As for her appearance, she's well proportioned and has dimples in her cheeks, round blue eyes, and wavy blond hair. She can talk English, which is a relief to me. I was afraid we'd have to converse in (High) German, which would have been hard. It's not the same as our Deitsch (Pennsylvania German, called Dutch). It's similar, but it takes time and concentration to understand each other.

Martha walked out to the barn first to see the animals, and she didn't just look at them—she patted them and talked to them. "I'm an animal lover," she said, "especially horses. Horseback riding is one of my favorite hobbies. I hope you have a horse here that I can ride."

I told her I don't think our driving horse has ever been ridden, but she went right into the stall with him, untied him, led him out, and jumped on his back. I gasped and told her to get down quickly. A horse that isn't used to being ridden sometimes bucks. But she just laughed and trotted him around the barnyard, riding bareback.

"This is a riding horse," she declared. "I can tell right

away. He must've been trained with riders before you had him." Then she dug her heels into his sides and galloped out the field lane and back, tail and mane and blond hair flying. It was obvious that she knew what she was doing, but it was still a relief to me when she got down.

We went into the house then, and I showed her to her room. As soon as she saw it, she cried, "Oh, I love this quaint old-fashioned room! What a lovely patchwork quilt this is on the bed!"

She went around the room looking at everything and exclaiming happily over it. She "just loved" the embroidered dresser scarves and the crocheted doily and pillowcase edging. It warmed my heart to see how delighted she was with everything.

Martha also fussed over the old hand pump in the washhouse and the big furnace kettle where we cook *Lattwarick* (apple butter). But the thing that fascinated her the most was the windmill. She changed into working clothes (slacks and a blouse) and promptly proceeded to climb the windmill, something we have forbidden our children to do. Nate sometimes climbs it when there's a fire in the neighborhood, to spot it.

I held my breath while she waved happily from the top, and then she climbed back down. My, what a spunky girl she is!

She's a willing worker, too. Martha helped to cut bunches of purple grapes for canning and washed all the dirty dishes. She says she wants to help in whatever we're doing and to learn how to do it, too.

Martha seems so eager and enthusiastic about everything. When the children came home from school, she made friends with them right away. She took them out into the yard and taught them a German game. Judging by the sounds that drifted in the window, she had them laughing and feeling at ease with her right off.

Nate and I watched from the kitchen window, and I commented to him that I'm glad she wears slacks, which are surely more modest for running around like that than a short skirt or short shorts would be.

He agreed but reminded me that the law of Moses says a woman should not wear man's clothing, nor should a man put on a woman's garment. "That's what pleases God. Women ought to wear decently long dresses and let the men wear the pants."

Later tonight Martha came to me and said, "I'd like to wear Amish clothes while I'm here. Would you show me what material to buy and lend me a pattern and show me how to make them?"

I was more than happy to comply. When Barbianne drove in tonight on the pony cart to meet the German girl and heard the story, she offered to let Martha use her patterns since they are about the same size.

So now Martha is planning to go over to Barbianne's house on Saturday. Barbianne will help her cut and sew her new clothes. I can hardly wait to see what she'll look like then! She will seem just like one of us. I wonder if she will want a *Kapp* (cap), too. ▓

September 12

*S*aturday evening. The work is all done, the house spick-and-span, the kitchen floor waxed and shiny, and the carriage washed—all ready for

Sunday. Church will be at Emanuel Yoder's tomorrow, and they will have the singing, too, in the evening.

Some of the fields of corn have been cut, and now it's cooler, too. There's a strong breeze blowing, and the windmill is pumping water for us again. The cistern has been nearly empty, but this will fill it up again. Fall is coming, and I am getting *gluschtich* (eager) to get the house-cleaning off the list so I can do things like piecing quilts and making rugs.

Nate is giving the boys haircuts, putting a bowl on top of their heads and snipping around it with a scissors. When he's done with them, I'll give him a haircut.

We had quite a surprise after supper. Sadie ran to the window and wondered, "Who's that walking in the lane?"

I peered out and answered, "It looks like it could be Rosemary." But I knew it couldn't be Rosemary.

Nate thought it might be Rosemary's sister Ruth. We all stood at the windows trying to figure out who it was. When she got closer, she smiled and waved her hand. Peter cried, "It's Martha!"

And it was Martha, neatly dressed in an Amish dress and apron and *Kapp*. We could hardly believe our eyes. What a difference it made in her appearance!

"How do you like them?" she asked when she walked into the kitchen. She whirled around in front of us.

Little Crist cried, "*Sie hot en Bopp!* (she has a hair roll)," and we all burst out laughing.

Martha explained, "Barbianne helped me to fix my hair this way instead of a ponytail. I like it better this way."

We all admired her. It made her look so homey and familiar.

"And guess what!" she went on, her eyes shining. "The

school teacher, Melvin Yoder, is taking me to the singing tomorrow evening. He said I can go with him if I wear Amish clothes. I can hardly wait to see what an Amish singing is like."

Peter asked, "Are you going along to church with us, too?"

"Oh yes. I'm hoping I'll be able to understand at least part of the sermon. I'm looking forward to that, too."

Well, well, I just hope it will be as interesting for her as she thinks it will be. I'm trying to figure out what my impression of our gatherings would be if I would be attending for the first time, or as seen through the eyes of a newcomer. Will she be impressed? ⊞

September 14

*M*onday. Martha came walking down the steps this morning, smiling and starry-eyed.

"How did you like it at the singing?" Sadie asked her first thing. "Did a boy ask to bring you home?"

Martha giggled. "Yes and no," she said. "After the singing was over, Melvin's sister Esther and I were walking out in the yard. Someone kept shining the beam of a flashlight into my face, and I couldn't see a thing.

"Esther whispered to me, 'That means someone wants to talk to you, maybe even to ask to take you home.' So I walked right up to where this guy was hiding behind a bush and told him I'm going home with Melvin Yoder." Her eyes twinkled mischievously.

"The poor boy," Nate moaned with a chuckle. "With your Amish clothes, he had no way of knowing you were not an Amish girl. He probably thought you were from another district and just starting to *rumschpringe* (run around with the young people) and wondered who the *shee Meedel* (pretty girl) is."

Martha nodded. "Could be. Not that I'm all that pretty though!" she added quickly.

Then she changed the subject. "Today I'm going to buy myself a bicycle, and then I'm going job hunting. Pamela Styer is going to help me get a job in town, close enough so I can go by bicycle every day. She'll be here at eight thirty to pick me up. I think I'd like to work in a sewing factory. Do any Amish girls work in garment factories?"

"A few do," I told her. "But mostly they take cleaning jobs or go along to market or work as a *Maut* (maid) for our own people. You could get a job going along to market on Fridays and Saturdays, but you have to get up early for that—as early as three or four in the morning. And they put in long days."

"I'll think about it," Martha said. "It would be worth it to work with other Amish girls. I think I'd like to sell things like homemade soft pretzels and shoofly pies."

When I was setting the table for breakfast, Martha asked, "Do you mind if I make breakfast this morning? I'd like to try one of my favorite recipes, a breakfast casserole."

I told her she surely may. Martha busily flitted around the kitchen, humming a merry little tune as she worked. She took out a casserole dish, and I'm not sure what all she put in besides lots of eggs, bread, cream, salt, and pepper.

This she put into the oven to bake. She was amazed at having to strike a match to light the gas oven (the pilot light conked out); she was used to an electric oven.

25

Next Martha sliced tomatoes and onions together and poured a dressing of sugar and vinegar over them. Then she picked up a scissors, went out to the flower bed, and cut a bouquet of marigolds and zinnias. She arranged them beautifully in a vase and set them on the middle of the table.

Martha put milk into a saucepan, brought it to a boil, added rolled oats, raisins, and English walnuts. It was a good breakfast, interesting and different from our usual fried eggs, mush, potatoes, and grapenuts or granola.

There are two things that she says she has to get used to here. One is that we don't use table napkins, and the other is that we use the same plates for our desserts that we used for the first course.

I told her to imagine the mother with ten children, twelve at her table three times a day. Two plates at a meal for each would be seventy-two in three meals, thirty-six extra plates to wash every day! She agreed that it was a time-saver.

Martha insisted on washing the breakfast dishes by herself and tidying up the kitchen before Pam came for her. I hope she finds a good job, for I think she will be a good dependable worker. ▦

October 1

Grandpa Dave and Grandma Annie came tonight to meet Martha. I think Dave really gets a kick out of her. They had things sounding rather lively with teasing and bantering back and forth. He won't outwit her right away; she has her tongue with her. Martha calls him Grampie, and Annie she calls Grammie. The children started to call them that now, too.

We've all grown fond of Martha since she's here. She says she likes it here and wants to stay five years! I told her she'll probably get married before that.

She said, "Nope, I'm not getting married before I'm twenty-five, and I'm not kidding—I mean it!" Martha's spunky, and I believe she does mean it. But, we'll see.

We made popcorn and brought in a gallon jug of cider. It's a time of year I like, when the trees are so colorful, and there's a tang in the air. Wild geese are winging their way southward, and the chrysanthemums are at their loveliest.

I'm still concerned about Henry and Priscilla. They haven't been here to visit since August. And I miss Dora so. All summer I was looking forward to when school starts so she would come home. But she didn't come home. Now I miss her a lot more than I did then.

All we see of Dora is at church and when we go to Henry's to visit. I'm afraid my fears weren't groundless. It makes me feel sad. I have to pray for God's will to be done, but it's not easy. My heart wants my own will to be done.
❈

October 8

We spent three days visiting friends and relatives in Summerville while Martha kept the home fires burning and the household running smoothly. Melvin and Rudy did the chores. Coming home was (as usual) the best part. "Be it ever so humble, there's no place like home" (Payne).

Home is a dear and pleasant place
Of family meals and friendly cheer,
And humble peacefulness and grace,
The fellowship of loved ones dear.

Nate is his kind-hearted self again since his cyst was removed, as helpful and understanding as he always was. Sometimes I have to wonder how he really would take it if Dora never came back to live with us. Maybe I would be the one that would have to comfort him yet.

This morning we had the first *Reife* (frost) of the season. It spites me to have the beautiful flowers frozen stiff and black, but I'm glad to be rid of the weeds. Fire in the wood stove feels good this morning. I'm drying yellow Delicious apple slices on the big *Daerrpann* (drying pan).

The children hunted their shoes out of the closets. Summer and barefooted days are over, autumn is here, and next will be winter.

On Tuesday evening Teacher Melvin was here for supper. The parents of the scholars take turns inviting him for a meal once a week. I can see why the children like him. He's an outgoing and interesting person. Later Nate said that Melvin knows so much about almost any subject you could mention, worldwide.

Much to Nate's delight, Melvin is an expert checker player. There aren't many people able to challenge Nate in that game! First, Melvin played a game of Dutch Blitz with the children and Martha. I think he had heard of Nate's status as a checker player and wanted to see what he could do. They are a good match for each other and were lost to the rest of us until bedtime.

Martha and Melvin have an agreement; he will teach

her to talk Deitsch (Pennsylvania German), and she'll teach him (High) German. Of course, he can read German from the Bible, but speaking it as an everyday language is something else.

Martha learns a lot from hearing us talking Deitsch and asking questions, but she'll still benefit from their biweekly lessons.

I don't think there will be any harm if they get together

like that. Martha has no intentions of joining the Amish, and Melvin is not the type that would fall for a non-Amish girl. He's sensible and levelheaded, and so is she. ▦

*S*aturday. We gathered all the large orange pumpkins and the tiny jack-be-littles and the green-and-white striped-neck pumpkins for pies. The golden maple leaves are falling everywhere. We rake them into huge piles. The children love to jump around in them.

Nate hitched the two big workhorses to the flatbed wagon. We all climbed on, and he drove out to the field. There we spent the afternoon picking up ears of corn that the harvester dropped. We threw them into the wagon. The horses start and stop on command, so no one has to stay on the wagon and hold the reins.

It's exhilarating to be able to see far and wide across the valley again and feel the refreshing wind sweeping by. We felt satisfaction in seeing the fat ears of corn flying through the air, and hearing them bounce against the bangboard as they filled the wagon bed. Flocks of raucous crows congregated in the trees in the fencerows and filled the air with their "caw, caw, caw!"

The crisp air and outdoor exercise sure works up an appetite. When the wind became chilly, we were all glad to be going in to supper fires and good things to eat.

Martha "just loved" it all. She declared, "Never before in my life have I enjoyed anything so much!"

I'm so glad she likes it here with us. We sure enjoy having her here, too. ▦

*G*loria Graham was here tonight once again, it had been quite awhile since she was here last. She's lonely again; George is away on a trip.

She settled herself into the Boston rocker with her knitting needles and her yarn. Gloria's making a little doggie jacket since George promised to buy her a little Pomeranian puppy on his way home.

I guess he felt a bit mean after all for making her choose between him and her Persian cat. A puppy will give her something to dote on when he's away.

Gloria hasn't said a word about me being fat since her apology, but she had something else on her mind tonight. "What I'd like to know is, why do you people wear such dark, drab, and dreary clothes? God made the sky a pretty blue, and his flowers are pink, red, and yellow, and all the colors of the rainbow. Surely God is a lover of beauty and color. Where do you read in the Bible that clothes should be black?"

She sure is outspoken! I told her, "We don't just wear black. We wear blue, green, purple, and burgundy, too."

"But you wear dark colors. Light-colored clothing isn't as depressing. You know, some white cakes are called angel food, and some chocolate cakes are called devil's food. I have a notion to buy you some light pink fabric, enough for you to sew a dress for yourself, and I want you to wear it, too. Make it with your usual pattern, nice and long, sleeves and a cape, so you can't say it's not modest.

"'There's nothing in your *Ordnung* (church rules) that says you can't wear a light pink dress, is there? Look out the window; see that pink glow in the west? Since God made the sky so colorful, why can't you wear a pink dress like that?"

I had an answer ready for her. "Can you imagine what that light pink dress would look like at the end of the day? After weeding a flower bed on hands and knees, picking berries or other produce, working in the barn and fields, or scrubbing the kitchen floor on hands and knees."

But Gloria wouldn't drop the subject. "You could wear an old work apron over the dress when you do a dirty job. Please just try it, won't you? Something light. It could be yellow, like a daffodil, or robin's-egg blue, if you like that better. I'd love to see you in it."

Funny Gloria! What will she think of next? What would be the use of sprucing up like that? Just to tease her, I told her I might become haughty and stuck-up then, if I'd wear such a dress.

When she was ready to leave, she said, "I'm going to knit you a white sweater for Christmas, and I want you to wear it, too."

I knew she didn't mean it, but I replied, "All right, if you make it soft enough, I'll wear it to bed. It might be just what I need for that below-zero weather."

With a wry face and a twinkle in her eye, she went out the door. I don't think she was offended, but with her, I never know. If she had been Pamela, I wouldn't worry a bit, but they're two different kinds. Oh well, she'll get over this hobby sometime, as before. ▦

*O*h my, such a lot has happened today! Church services were at neighbor Eli's, and a visiting couple from Maine showed up. They were Pam's guests; she brought them with permission from Eli's.

Preacher Emanuel had the text. When he saw four *Englischer* (non-Amish) there, he used a few English sentences in his sermon. Martha can't understand much of the sermon yet either if it's not in English.

This was unusual, and I don't think anyone fell asleep as he preached. People really sat up and listened. There were quite a few frowns from the older members.

Near the end of the services, Preacher Emanuel asked the other ministers to give a testimony to the sermon, supply anything that should have been said, and correct any mistakes. They rebuked him for deviating from our "mother tongue," which they said is so necessary to keep us separate from the ways of the world.

Henry became upset, and he and Priscilla left before dinner was served. Tonight they paid us a visit and explained their motives clearly. Now we know why they wooed Dora from us and why Henry was teaching Priscilla and Dora another language.

Henry was really wound up tonight. "How can people be so stiff-necked and hard-hearted?" he asked, his eyes blazing with intensity. "How could they rebuke Emanuel for sharing God's word with outsiders in a language they can understand?"

I started to say, "The visitors probably just came out of curiosity." But Henry silenced me with a withering look before I could finish.

Nate suggested, "Emanuel could have talked to them all afternoon, sharing God's word with them in English then."

However, Henry wasn't listening. He had something else he wanted to say. Priscilla came and stood by his side, and he quietly announced, "From now on, Dora is our daughter."

We two couples stood there, facing each other, and I felt stunned and dazed. The first thought that entered my mind was, why do we have to go through this yet, too? First we have to bear the pain of parting with Amanda, and now we lose Dora, too.

The children were romping happily on the lawn; I heard Dora laughing with them. I cried out, "But you gave Dora to us. She's ours!"

Henry shook his head. "I made a mistake when I said you could raise Dora. I didn't realize how much that hurt Priscilla and what a struggle she had to accept that decision."

He clasped Priscilla's hand and said, "Dora is our daughter, and we'll take the matter to court if necessary."

There was such a note of finality in his voice that I knew there wasn't a whisper of a chance that he would change his mind. Nate realized it, too, for he turned away with a stricken look on his face and headed for the barn.

"Wait!" Henry called. "Come back. We have something else to say."

When Nate returned, he said, "Today we have decided to answer God's call. We are going to Africa to take the word of God there. In other words, be missionaries. I've been in Africa twice, and I felt the need there. We're leav-. ing as soon as we can make all the arrangements. A Mennonite mission board wants to send us."

It was a good thing that I was sitting down; the news was such a shock. Africa! So far away! And Dora was going with them! They were leaving the Amish church! It just didn't fully sink in right away.

Nate told Henry, "Don't you remember what you said when you were recovering from your truck accident? You felt that it was a chastening from God, that it helped you to give up your own selfish will."

Henry nodded. "I still feel that way. I was hankering after freedom to serve the flesh. But this is different. Now my desire is to serve God and go wherever he leads me. I don't desire to have more of things of the world or more luxuries. It won't be an easy life there in Africa. We'll have to live with less material things than we have now."

"Does . . . does Dora really want to go along?" I asked weakly, desperately hoping that there just might be a chance that she would want to stay with us.

Priscilla nodded and said, "I am so thankful that she chose to go with us. Words just can't express—" Tears filled her eyes.

At that moment, it didn't seem so impossible for me to give up Dora anymore, for I realized that Priscilla needed her more than I did. After they left, I wandered off along the creek and had a good cry. I'm afraid things will never be the same again. Our happy times together . . . I'm afraid those days are over forever.

Life is hard sometimes. Will I ever again be able to enjoy to the fullest the changes of the seasons and country living, knowing that Henry and Priscilla and Dora and the little girls are in such a faraway land, maybe even among hostile people?

Nate was quiet and withdrawn and ate no more than a few bites for supper. He shared the most sobering thought of all: "After they leave, will we ever see them again?"

Our prayers will go with them continually, and our trust in the help of God will calm us and soothe us, I'm sure. But it's still so hard to see them go. ✠

October 29

I had a letter from Polly today. Dear Polly . . . so wise and helpful. Her letters always arrive just when we need them most. How does she know?

At the beginning of her letter, she had written the Serenity Prayer: "Lord, help me to accept the things I cannot change, to change the things I can, and the wisdom to know the difference."

Polly wrote, "The presence of Christ brings us the peace that passes all understanding. He instills in us this assurance: if we abide in his love, no adversary can pluck us out of his hand. Christ's generous heart seeks to grant us the serenity of soul that gives our lives joy and peace, even in the midst of adversity.

"This is a comforting thought, but knowing these things is not enough. We have to apply them to our lives, too, and to take time to instill them into our hearts."

I know it's true. The help is there, and if we ask, we shall receive. ✠

*W*hether serene or not, life goes on, we've found. Henry's will not be leaving before spring, so we'll make the most of the time we have left.

It seems hard now when we invite them over for a meal. Henry and Priscilla have to eat at a little table by themselves. They have been put in the ban, disfellowshipped by their own choosing.

Whenever they leave for home, I feel overwhelmed by a bleak feeling. Are they really sure that's what they should do? What if Dora becomes headstrong and rebellious there in a strange country? What if she runs away or does something rash? All kinds of fears and worries assail me.

I'm so glad that Martha is here. She's like a golden sunbeam in our home—a ray of sunshine to brighten our days. When she comes riding in the lane on her bicycle, home from the sewing factory, she brings cheer along. The children love her; she entertains them a lot.

Teacher Melvin comes twice a week for their exchange of language lessons, and the house rings with hilarity then. Oh, the gaiety and optimism of youth! It's like a breath of fresh air when one is feeling jaded, weary, or disillusioned. Their colorful, pithy ideas and remarks add spice and interest. It's great having young people in the house! ⚼

November 11

*W*e spent the day helping neighbor Eli's family get ready for Hannah's wedding. Pam told me awhile ago already that she'd like to have the Amish wedding roast recipe, so I copied it down for her:

Amish Wedding Roast

30 capons, roasted, deboned, and cut into small pieces

30 gallons bread cubes	5 dozen eggs, beaten
4 gallons celery, ground	7 teaspoons pepper
7 lbs. butter	14 tablespoons salt
broth, as needed	1 cup chopped parsley

Melt butter, and add the ground celery. Cook until celery is soft. Cool. Beat eggs, and add the salt, pepper, and parsley. Pour over the bread cubes and mix well. Add the celery and butter mixture. Add broth if needed. Mix with the meat, and roast until done. Serves 350 people.

Pam stopped in tonight. She's quite excited that she is invited to the wedding tomorrow. She said she can't believe her good fortune. She'd been hoping for the chance to attend an Amish wedding for quite awhile. And Martha is even more excited about it than Pam, if possible. I hope they enjoy it as much as they think they will. ✷

November 12

*H*annah and Ben's wedding day. I was surprised to see Gloria and George here, too. Gloria came over to me in the morning to ask a few questions about our traditions. "I've heard so much about these Amish weddings, and I can't believe I'm actually attending one."

Then Gloria asked, "Is it true that you have such a big

feast and eat so much that you all have to go to the drug-store the next day for something for your indigestion?"

My mouth dropped, I'm afraid, and I mumbled, "Well, if any eat too much, it's their own fault."

It wonders me: What all is being said about the Amish that isn't true? Yet maybe we deserved that. I guess it really wouldn't be necessary to have such a big meal. A small meal like we serve after church services would suffice. But would it seem like a wedding without the feast? After all, Jesus went to a wedding feast.

In pondering it later, I concluded that hardworking folks can take a day of feasting in stride. But it's true that a lot of these things are not given much thought until they are questioned by outsiders.

Maybe we think too much *sel is wie es immer waar* (that's the way it always was). But we have to be careful that we aren't drifting into worldly and sinful ways before we are aware of it. ✳

November 13

*M*artha was bubbling over with enthusiasm this morning, about the wedding yester-day. She said she loved every minute of it. Melvin took her to the supper table, and there was some whistling after-ward. But they both got the point across quite plainly that no one was to get such ideas, for there's nothing to it. They're not a pair.

Martha is happy with the way she is being accepted by the *Yunge* (youths) even though she has no intentions of joining. With her Amish clothes and *Kapp*, the casual observer couldn't tell the difference. But no one takes her seriously, knowing she will remain an outsider.

Tonight I finally found out (through Martha) about Pamela's religion. She's a Catholic! So that's where she has been going when we see her passing early on some mornings—to mass. But I have to wonder how staunch a Catholic she is—or are divorces allowed nowadays?

I've been thinking about these different religions. If people are sincere and diligent in what they've been taught, will that be good enough for them? Or, even though they're sincere, might they be sincerely wrong? Does Pam feel that way about us? It's all too deep for me.

As for Martha, she said, "I'm still seeking. I want to learn all about the different religions before I make a commitment." She told me that she's doing a study on Mormonism now, and that next she wants to learn about the Jehovah's Witnesses—whoever they are!

This troubles me. I know it's all too easy for a young person to be deceived or led on wrong paths. We must pray for her, that she will know and believe that our lives can have no foundation except that which is laid in Jesus Christ as Lord. ✷

Thanksgiving Day

*T*his is the day the *Englischer* ancestors set apart to remember to give thanks to God for a bountiful harvest yield, for ample food and provisions. It's also a day for our people to pause and think of our blessings and, as on every day, thank God for them.

Grandpa Dave and Grandma Annie, Rudy and Barbianne, and Henry and Priscilla, and of course Melvin, were here for dinner. Melvin seems almost like a member of the family lately.

Martha made the Amish roast, with filling and turkey together, with Grandma Annie's experienced guidance. Everyone seemed lighthearted and cheerful. It would have been a perfect day if it hadn't been for the little table set for Henry and Priscilla to eat separately.

Sometimes I feel like smashing that little table to bits. Then I feel guilty for having such thoughts. I know the ordinance of shunning is in the *Ordnung*, but they aren't drunkards or idolaters or such.

Martha kindly took her plate and sat at the little table with Henry and Priscilla. The conversation there was livelier than at the big table!

In the afternoon big flakes of beautiful snow began to waft earthward. Nate and Melvin played checkers while the other men looked on and cheered for them. We womenfolk discussed things like quilt making and housecleaning and child raising.

Barbianne is once again hoping and dreaming, but her hopes are veiled with a shadow: memory of the little waxen form in the tiny coffin. We hope and pray that all will be well this time.

It was a beautiful Thanksgiving Day. In looking back over the past year, Nate and I have a special reason to be grateful and to give thanks. I hope we never again take the blessings of good health for granted.

O give thanks unto the Lord; for he is good;
for his mercy endures forever. ▒

Our winter weather didn't last long. Now we're having a week of Indian summer.

I appreciate the mellow ripeness of autumn after that bit of winter we had. A chilly wind had swept down from the mountains. It whined through the chimney and made the windmill creak and groan. A mixture of cold rain and snow flurries brought down the last of the leaves.

However, the sunshine and warmth of today and yesterday beckoned me outdoors. I decided to go to a garage sale in the neighborhood. I do love going to garage sales, but at this one I was thoroughly humiliated and wished I hadn't gone.

It was advertised in the paper as starting at eight in the morning. As I usually do, I decided to go an hour earlier, thinking that all the bargains would be sold away if I didn't. I set the table for breakfast, then grabbed my bonnet, got out the scooter, and was on my merry way.

As I had expected, at the sale a half dozen women were already sorting through the displays. I happily picked up a stainless steel teakettle, the kind I wanted for quite awhile already. I found some shiny, new-looking bread pans, a bag of pieces of leftover fabric that would be excellent to use for quilt making, a toy horse for Crist, and a few nice crocheted doilies.

I was rejoicing at having found all these bargains and saving money. But when I went over to the table to pay for my armloads, I overheard someone saying in a low voice, "Look at what all that woman got. These Amish women are always the first ones at a sale, too."

I hung my head in shame and slunk away. That cured

me from rushing after bargains. Catch me going to a garage sale again! After this I'll leave the best deals for someone else, I told myself. But how long will I be able to keep that promise?

At the end of the drive, I met Priscilla coming in on a bicycle! It didn't help my feelings any when she said, "Oh, Miriam, it looks like you already found all the bargains! Maybe I should go home."

However, the sight of her riding a bicycle was such a shock and surprise to me that I, to my dismay, had a wild desire to burst out laughing. Imagine that!

Will I ever get used to seeing Priscilla zooming up and down the hills on a bicycle? It was the first time I saw an "Amish" woman riding a bicycle, but I really don't suppose that it's any sillier than how I look riding a scooter on the road.

Priscilla didn't seem to notice my reaction. She began telling me about the unhappy experience she and Henry had yesterday when they went shopping at the bulk food store, which is Amish owned. They apparently didn't realize or else forgot that the *Meiding* (shunning) would be practiced there, too.

When they came through the checkout with their loaded cart, the Amish clerk refused to wait on them, saying she wouldn't be allowed to take their money. Finally she went to the back room to consult with the boss.

When she came back, she said that if they'd lay the money on the counter instead of putting it directly into her hand, it would be okay.

Poor Priscilla! But that is what they chose, and nothing that anyone would say could dissuade them. ⌗

A blanket of beautiful snow is covering every flaw and imperfection on the farm. Martha loves snow. She took the children outside and had a lively snowball battle with them. Then she taught them to make snow sculptures, and now a Papa Bear, Mama Bear, and Baby Bear stand along the front walk, guarding the yard.

They came trooping inside, all rosy-cheeked and merry. Peter happily announced, "We're going to chop down a Christmas tree to decorate. I'm going to pick out the prettiest one."

Little Crist demanded, "Find the ax!"

Sadie, her eyes shining, was jumping up and down in her eagerness. "I'm going to string popcorn to put on the tree and make a colored chain for it."

I thought, Oh dear! Martha must have put them up to this. How will I explain to her that Amish people don't decorate trees for Christmas?

I fled out to the barn and found Nate. He came in and explained it kindly to her. He mentioned what it says in Jeremiah, about the heathen cutting a tree out of the forest and decking it with silver and gold.

We don't take everything in the Old Testament as seriously as what the New Testament says, since we are no longer under the law. But God had good reasons for the rules and the law. We certainly don't want to seem to be worshiping an idol instead of the living God.

At first Martha looked puzzled, but she gave in gracefully. The children reluctantly gave up the idea, too. They were happy again when I told them they could help make peanut butter balls to dip in melted chocolate. Martha asked if she could make "saint hearts" (sand tarts).

Soon the kitchen was filled with good smells, and everyone seemed happy again. The Christmas presents are all wrapped and waiting, on the sideboard in the sitting room (instead of under a tree). I wonder, How did bringing in a tree and decorating it ever become associated with celebrating Christ's birth? ❄

*Z*ero degrees this morning! Our carriage wheels screeched and sang in the frozen snow on the road on the way to church services. On the back roads, sleighing would have gone better, but the main roads are bare.

As we drove through town, we passed a *Karich* (church building with a steeple), and I saw the elegant architecture and the beautiful stained-glass windows. I wondered what it would seem like to belong to such a church. Once I was in a *Karich*, to attend an elderly neighbor lady's funeral. I was awed by the high domed ceiling, soft thick carpeting on the floor, the cushioned pews, the beautiful soft music, and the trained voices in the choir.

I had to wonder, What if they had church services in their homes and had to sit on backless benches for several hours? I think it's easier to have warm fellowship when we meet in a home. That's how the early Christians met, and we've always done it that way, too.

How much money is piled up in bricks and stone, for buildings unused most of the week? What if all the money that built fancy churches across America were used to feed the hungry or to build decent houses for the poor? ▦

December 24

*L*ast evening Martha had a surprise planned for the children, never once realizing that Nate and I would not be positively delighted, too. She had invited Teacher Melvin over. We were all sitting around the kitchen table, singing Christmas carols, when the door burst open. With a loud "HO, HO, HO, Merry Christmas to all," a jolly fat man dressed in Santa Claus clothes came in. He handed out presents to each of the children. Dora was here, too, because Henry and Priscilla are on a trip.

Martha bustled around, making and serving hot chocolate and cookies. "Santa Claus" was one of her friends from the sewing factory.

After Santa left, Little Crist said reproachfully to me, "I thought you said there was no Santa Claus."

I told him that it was just a man dressed in Santa Claus clothes. Nate explained to Martha that we don't believe in teaching children that Santa is a big elf who lives at the North Pole. If we deceived them like that, they might think that God is only a myth, too. We are careful to not give them coloring books or greeting cards with Santa Claus on. Instead, we celebrate the birth of Christ.

Martha apologized later. But there was nothing to forgive; we knew she meant it well.

After the younger children were in bed, Nate and Melvin were still playing checkers in the sitting room, with Martha watching and cheering. I was able to have a heart-to-heart chat with Dora once again out in the kitchen. I asked her about the upcoming trip to Africa and whether she really wanted to go.

She hesitated a bit, then said yes. A bit wistfully, she added, "I'd like so stay here, too."

That reopened the wound in my heart. In these past months, it has been such a struggle to accept that Dora is leaving. No matter how often I think I've gained the victory over self, I find that I have to seek it over and over again.

I've been consoling myself with the thought that maybe when the time actually comes to leave, Dora will choose to stay after all. I know that Priscilla and Henry have glamorized going as missionaries so much that Dora doesn't yet realize what it will mean for her to leave us all.

However, I don't want to be selfish, for I know Priscilla needs her and wants her as much as I do. I pray for God's protecting hand to be over them all when they leave. ✳

December 31

*I*t's five years since our little Amanda entered the gloryland. She is Peter's twin and was born with glutaric aciduria. This is a day for strengthened hope and faith's renewing. We know that our departed loved one does not lie asleep, but is even now in God's presence.

I have to think back to that time, and also to Rudy and Barbianne's loss. I remember how hurt Barbianne was when her first child was stillborn, and when Grandma Annie told her that her baby was better off dead. And yet I have to believe that Amanda is better off in her heavenly home, with Jesus, than in this sinful world.

Sometimes I think it would be easier to know that Dora is safe in heaven than in faraway Africa, where there are many evils and dangers. Maybe I have magnified these things out of proportion to the risks. But one of my greatest concerns is that she might be deceived or led astray. At other times I fear that we will never see her again.

I cling to the words of Jesus: "I will not leave you comfortless: I will come to you." If we abide in Christ, we can claim this precious promise. ✳

Testings

※ ※ ※ ※ ※ ※ ※ ※ ※ ※ ※

January 1

*T*he New Year has begun.
The mercies of the Lord are new every morning. I like to
think that the dawning of New Year's Day is the time to be
forgetting those things that are behind, forgetting our past
failures and mistakes. It is a reminder that as far as the east
is from the west, so far has God removed our transgres-
sions from us. We are given time to press forward toward
the mark for the prize of the high calling of God in Jesus
Christ.

We've noticed some strange goings-on these past few
days. Nate says that Mazie, our tamest cow, has been giving a lot less milk. I discovered that a pan of homemade
Pannhaas (scrapple) I had set in the washhouse to cool
was gone!

Then as I was putting up last year's calendar pictures
out in the *Heisli* (outhouse), I noticed that the devotional
books I keep out there on a ledge were missing. (We have
a bathroom in the house, too, but never tore down the
outhouse. Some of us still prefer it instead of the bathroom; it comes in handy when we have a lot of visitors.)

Well, at least whoever took them should find some
spiritual help. They were a New Testament, *Streams in the
Desert*, and *The Imitation of Christ*. As for the milk and
Pannhaas, if they're hungry, they're welcome to it. But it

wonders me so much who would be hungry enough to take milk from a cow.

The thought of someone being in our washhouse at night isn't comforting. Let's hope it was just a tramp or a drifter passing through.

I asked Martha if she knows anything about it, and she was as mystified as we were. I thought maybe she took the books out of the outhouse, but she said she didn't. And the children claim innocence, too. It sure is a mystery! ⌗

January 6

*T*his morning I found the New Testament back on the shelf in the outhouse, and inside was a ten-dollar bill! That sure beats all! Apparently someone took the food and paid for it! If they have money to pay for food, why wouldn't they go to a grocery store? It sure is strange.

Yesterday I made five shoofly pies and put them on the table in the washhouse to cool. I was going to bring them in last night but forgot it. This morning there were only four left. Mazie the cow is still giving less milk every day. But as far as we know, nothing was taken but food, besides the devotional books, which are all back in place.

So whoever it was is still around! We're puzzled and uneasy. I guess we'll have to tell Teacher Melvin about it and get his brains working on the case. Maybe he can solve the mystery for us.

Melvin is an excellent teacher. He makes school really interesting for the children. Last week one morning, Little Crist came downstairs with a hoarse cough. I could tell that he was sick, but he insisted that he was well enough to go to school. He couldn't eat a bite for breakfast, and he sat by the stove shivering. When Nate told him he couldn't go to school today, he cried *vun Hatze* (from the heart), pitifully. That shows how much he likes school.

The Deitsch-German lessons between Melvin and Martha are progressing nicely, too. It goes faster because there are a lot of similarities: our Pennsilfaanisch Deitsch is a dialect of German. The two students are quick at *Lanning* (learning) and have a lot of fun practicing their conversation.

Melvin can now speak (High) German fairly well, and Martha is getting better every day at Deitsch and at understanding the sermons at church. She's seeming more and more like one of the family, making herself at home so well here. ✳

January 8

*M*ore snow on top of the frozen snow on the ground. That makes ideal sleighing weather. Martha loves to go sleighing, and Melvin has his big bobsled at Rudy's place. Tonight he hitched the two big workhorses to it and took us all for a ride. What fun!

The air was so clear and frosty, and the twinkling stars again seemed so close that we felt like reaching out and touching them. We were warm and cozy, huddled under the carriage robes on back.

Melvin started the song "It Came Upon A Midnight Clear," and we all joined in, not caring that the time for singing Christmas carols was past. Sadie slipped her hand into mine, and I squeezed it, keenly aware that she's the only little girl we have left.

My heart ached from realizing that and from the beauty of the song and the loveliness of the starry night. When we drove back into the barnyard, I happened to glance up toward the upper barn window. For an instant, I thought I saw a light flicker on and then off again—like the beam of a flashlight.

When I said something about it to Nate, he just laughed and joked, "You must have stars in your eyes tonight!"

Was it actually a light in the barn, just the reflection of another light from afar, or maybe even a moonbeam? I keep thinking about that missing food and milk. What if someone is using our barn for a hideout? ▦

January 11

*W*e found twin heifer calves in the barn this morning, much to Martha's delight. She's usually out in the barn helping with the chores whenever it's possible, for she's a great animal lover.

Martha talks to the horses, pats their necks, and they talk back to her, in horse language, nickering softly. She likes to feed them each an apple. She can't pass by any of the cows without calling them by name and patting them. The barn cats swarm around her, too, for she's the only one who gives them attention.

When she came upon those two little newborn calves, she was oohing and aahhing over them so much that I thought she'd forgotten all about going to her job. But just a few minutes before it was time to leave, she dashed into the house, washed her hands, ran a brush through her hair, and grabbed a bite to eat.

She rushed out the door just as Melvin drove in the lane for her. I hope her co-workers won't detect a barnyard smell on her. During this snowy weather, Melvin drives her to work in the one-horse sleigh, then goes to pick her up again in the evening after school.

She asked him to do that and offered to pay him, but of course he said he'd do it without pay. I think he enjoys her company, but who wouldn't? She's so lively and interesting.

I wonder when Melvin will start taking a girl home from the singing, besides Martha. Maybe by spring, if the little rhyme I saw in *Die Botschaft* is true.

> When April showers bring May flowers,
> And tulips by the dozen,
> A boy starts thinking of a girl,
> One that's not his cousin.

—*Unknown* ⌗

January 13

*R*udy came over in person this morning to bring us the happy news. They have a baby son! It was two years ago in August that they buried a stillborn son, so this is truly a cause for rejoicing.

According to Rudy, he is healthy, a fine big *Buppeli*, delivered at home with the help of a midwife. I had to go over right away this afternoon to see Barbianne and the newborn child for myself.

A gladder, happier set of parents you could not find! Barbianne sat up in bed, holding her baby and exclaiming over him. "Look at these perfect little patties (hands). See, he clasps my finger already! And his knees are cute and dimpled." She took off one of his booties and caressed his toes.

I had to laugh at her. She was just like a little girl with a new doll.

"He looks just like Rudy," she marveled. "His nose and chin especially." She kissed him on the forehead, then handed him to me to hold, saying, "I'm so happy! I don't think I'll be able to sleep a wink tonight."

However, later she admitted that she was exhausted, so I stayed and cared for Baby James. She took a long nap. Her *Maut* couldn't come until tonight.

Rudy came in and held little James while I prepared supper. He was about as bad as Barbianne, talking baby talk and fussing over the baby. It does my heart good though, to see how they love him.

I remember how Rudy always had a kind word for Amanda and how he used to lift her up into the air and call her his Mandy girl. He always liked children, and I'm sure he will make a good dad.

When Melvin came back from taking Martha home on the sleigh, I was just going out the walk, so he offered to drive me home yet, too. I gratefully accepted.

On the way home, I told Melvin about the food missing from the washhouse and Mazie's milk shortage. I reported that I thought I saw a light in the upper barn window.

Melvin was astonished and said he would like to make a thorough search of our barn sometime. What if there's another Oscar Thompson around? Oscar had posed as a harmless old man seeking to join the Amish. Then later we found out that he was a criminal and wanted by the police. Such a mystery gives me the shivers. ▓

*O*ur no-church Sunday. This forenoon Nate read Bible stories to the children. I was reading *Our Daily Bread*. It is rather sobering to know that the reflection of our lives can be either a stumbling block to others, or like a spiritual glow, lighting their way in the footsteps of Christ and to the honor and glory of God.

This afternoon Martha made more snow sculptures for the children, and this time it was cows! They even looked surprisingly real.

Melvin came over this afternoon to search the barn but found nothing strange except for a few Twinkies wrappers in the haymow and a spoon on a ledge. If anyone has been using our barn as a hideout, they must've left for the day, or for good, we hope. It is all very puzzling.

Tonight I was reading an article about Claas Epp Jr., a Russian Mennonite farmer of the 1870s. He led a group of followers by wagon train and by camel on a tragic trek eastward across Russia. They were searching for the City of Refuge, to await the return of Jesus to set up a kingdom here on the earth.

Claas was dressed in robes, expecting to ascend to heaven bodily on the date that he thought had been revealed to him (in 1889). When Jesus did not come then, he changed the date to 1891. Once again it was a lesson for all that no one knows, nor is anyone able to predict, just when the return of Christ will be.

There was even an Amish man, Jonas Stutzman near Walnut Creek, Ohio, who set the date for Christ's return in 1852. He wore only white clothes, and therefore they called him Der Weiss (The White) Stutzman. In preparation for the event, he built an oversized chair for Jesus to sit on. Jonas wrote a booklet about the return of Christ and the date that had been revealed to him.

There have been others, too, who thought it had been revealed to them just when Christ would come again. But no one has ever had it right. It's not important for us to know when it will be if we live so as to be ready for the midnight cry, "Behold, the bridegroom comes." ❄

January 25

*T*onight before supper I sent Peter to the cellar for a can of dark sweet cherries. He came back up two steps at a time, frightened and hollering, "There's a man in the cellar!" His eyes were huge, and he was trembling, so I knew he wasn't pretending.

"Th—there's a m-man in the cellar," he said, stuttering from surprise. "He h-hid behind the p-potato bin."

Nate had just come in for supper, with the gas lantern he used in the barn still in his hand. He suggested, "Maybe you just saw your own shadow."

"No, I'm sure it was someone," Peter cried. "When he saw me, he went 'oooh' and disappeared behind the bin.

We should go to the phone shanty and call the police!"

"First we'll take a look in the cellar," Nate said.

He bravely marched down the broad stone steps with the lantern. I followed fearfully with the flashlight. First thing, we noticed that the outside cellar door was open. Cautiously we peered behind the potato bin, in the coal bin, and in every dark corner, but found no one.

Nate went up the outside steps, looked around, and called down, "There are tracks in the snow leading away from the cellar door. I'm going to follow them."

I was scared to wait alone in the cellar, so I decided to grab a can of cherries and go back to the kitchen. But there was not a single can of sweet cherries left! The shelves were still full of sour cherries, but no sweets. Our tree didn't give much last summer, but I was sure there were at least ten quarts left. And now they had all disappeared.

Suddenly I got an eerie feeling as if someone were watching me, and I raced up the steps almost as fast as Peter had, with the dread that someone might be following me and could grab me from behind any second.

The children were standing at the top of the steps, peering down and looking as frightened as I felt. I told them there was no one in the cellar and laughed to put them at ease. But I did firmly hook the cellar door shut.

When Nate came back in, he spoke to me in a low voice so the children wouldn't hear. The tracks leading away from the cellar door went out to the road and then disappeared into the darkness.

It made me feel so jittery that I almost decided not to go visit the *Heisli* tonight. When I did get up enough spunk to go, I took the New Testament from the little shelf and opened it, intending to read a few verses by flashlight.

There, inside, was another ten-dollar bill! I sure got out of there in a hurry!

Martha was spending the evening at Rudy's place. I told Nate, "It makes me feel nervous to think of her walking home alone in the dark. Would you please hitch up and bring her home with the horse?"

"Don't you worry," he told me. "Melvin will bring her home in the sleigh."

Now it's bedtime, and she's still not back, I doubt that I'll be able to sleep until she's safe in the house. The windmill is creaking and whining eerily, and I can't stop my mind from churning over the thought of someone hiding in our cellar.

Nate assured me, "Don't worry. It's probably just a mischievous boy. Don't you remember how frightened you were last winter when we thought we had a prowler in the house? Then it turned out to be just Franie walking in her sleep! Relax now, come to bed, and sleep."

I wish I'd have the calm nature he has. ▦

January 26

*L*ast night after I went to bed, I did fall asleep. But several hours later something woke me, and I sat up in bed to listen. I heard a bump, and then I thought I heard voices.

I wakened Nate, and we quickly got dressed. He cautiously opened the kitchen door a crack. When he saw that there was a light in the kitchen and heard Martha's voice, he opened the door wide.

There sitting at the table were Martha and Melvin and a

strange young man. We stood there blinking in surprise.

Martha said, "Come and meet our guest, Marc Wellington."

Marc stood and greeted us politely, extending his hand for a handshake.

Martha had made some hot chocolate and was passing a plate of cookies, so we sat down at the table, too.

"Marc needs a place to stay tonight," Melvin explained, "so I told him he could go home with me to Rudy's place. They have several empty rooms upstairs."

I studied the young man and liked what I saw. He looked decent, not the long-haired hippie type. His eyes were thoughtful under well-shaped brows and a high forehead.

"Where are you from?" Nate asked Marc, by way of striking up a conversation.

"Originally I'm from Colorado. But I'm on a two-year assignment as a missionary in this area."

Well! I thought. Henry and Priscilla are going to Africa to be missionaries, and this young man comes here.

But when he told us he was a Mormon, I could understand. Their beliefs are so different from ours.

Martha was enthused. "That's great! I'm studying about your faith just now. I never thought I'd get to meet one of you people in person."

Melvin got up then and declared, "It's time for school teachers and hardworking folks to get to bed. Let's go."

Marc thanked Martha courteously for the cookies, and they left.

"Where did you find him?" Nate wondered. "Was he going from door to door, doing missionary work?"

Martha shook her head. "We were driving home from

Rudy's in the sleigh, and when we were nearly home, we passed him walking along the road. When we turned in our lane here, he followed us and asked if we know of a place where he could stay tonight.

"He seemed so well-mannered and polite that I trusted him right away and suggested that he could go with Melvin to Rudy's place. I thought they would be sure to give him a room. Do you think they'll mind?"

"They probably won't know a thing about it until morning," Nate replied. "But you can't tell much about a person from one conversation with him. How could you be sure he's to be trusted?

"Ordinarily we aren't quick to take someone into our home when we know next to nothing about him. How do you know he's telling the truth when he says he's a missionary?"

"Oh, I know he's to be trusted!" Martha cried. "I could tell right away. I just know he's a fine young man. I'd like to get to know him better."

"It would be better if you didn't," I told Martha, feeling it necessary to warn her to be careful about forming a friendship with him. "Their beliefs are so different from ours."

"Yeah, different from *yours*," Martha replied saucily. "You know I didn't commit myself to anything yet."

She got up. "It's time I get to bed, too. Goodnight." She tiptoed up the stairs.

"*Ach mei!* (oh my)," Nate said. "Just what made her so spunky? Why does she resent it that we warned her about befriending that young man, Marc?"

I shook my head. "We'd better be careful what we say or we'll just make her defensive. I'm surprised at Martha."

This morning when Martha got up, she told us why. In spite of having gotten to bed late, she was up early, preparing one of her famous breakfast casseroles, singing while she worked. She put a Sunday tablecloth on the table, got out the company dishes and our best china, and put a green-vined house plant on the table as a centerpiece.

"What are you celebrating?" I asked curiously. "Or have you invited company for breakfast?"

"Marc's coming," she said simply. "I told him to come here for breakfast."

"But . . . but . . . ," I sputtered.

Martha cut in. "Don't say another word. Let me tell you something—Marc is the man I'm going to marry. I knew it the minute I first met him. It was love at first sight."

"What! Does he know it?" I asked in amazement. I had never heard of such a thing before.

Martha burst out laughing. "Of course he doesn't, at least not yet. But I'm not going to waste any time before I make him aware of it."

"But you don't know anything about him," I protested. "What if he has a wife, or even several wives, where he came from? Isn't that one of their customs?"

Martha burst out laughing again. "Of course I wouldn't marry him if he already has a wife! That would be against the law. But I know Marc is single. And I don't want you to say another word to me about Marc's religion. Promise me you won't! I want to find out the truth by myself without having to listen to prejudice against them."

Before I could reply, the door opened, and Nate came in. He was followed by Marc, who greeted me with a pleasant good morning and greeted Martha warmly as well. Martha was a gracious hostess as she served her casserole and fried mush and *Pannhaas* (scrapple) and then her delicious oatmeal and raisins cooked in milk.

Marc did full justice to the meal, commenting on how good a home-cooked meal tasted once again.

It's easy to understand why Martha fell for Marc. One can't help but like him. As for me being prejudiced against his religion, I'll have to tell Martha that I'm not. It's just that I don't know much at all about Marc's faith. I just want her to be careful. We've all grown very fond of her since she's here and don't want her to be misled in any way. ▓

February 3

*I*n my *Musings of a Housewife* book, it says a kitchen should be a sacred place of reverence where the fragrance of newly baked bread mingles with contentment and peace so beautiful and serene that all who dwell there are filled with joy and happiness.

Well! How can I keep the kitchen a place of peace and reverence? It's the only well-heated room in the house unless we have company. So the kitchen is the center of activity and hubbub. When the weather is bad, the mats are full of rows of boots, and there are wet mittens on the stovepipe shelf.

When it's really cold outside, everyone crowds around the stove. When they're hungry, the center of attraction is the table or the gas refrigerator.

Tonight, in the midst of the flurry of getting on overcoats, caps, boots, and mitts for choring, Pamela popped in. She asked me to hem up a skirt for her and stayed to visit until it was done.

I suppose Pam's little kitchen always stays neat and clean, but she doesn't seem to mind the clutter here. She said she came across an old Amish proverb: Eat it up, wear it out, make it do, or do without.

That set me to thinking. Although being thrifty is part of our heritage, some of the things we used to regard as luxuries are accepted as necessities nowadays. ▦

February 5

G loria Graham stopped in tonight to show us her new Pomeranian puppy that George bought for her. She's every bit as silly over it as she was over her cat!

Says she, "Would you like to hold Itsy Bitsy Weeums Doggie Luv?"

The puppy has a long, sophisticated name that I can't remember, but she calls him Itsy Bitsy. Thankfully, Gloria didn't mention a pink dress or white sweater again. She chatted for about twenty minutes, then left again, friendly as could be.

Tonight Martha came home from Rudy's and announced that there will be a spelling bee for adults at school on Friday evening. She coaxed Melvin into making one for the parents and anyone else who wants to come.

Marc got a special invitation from her. She's a good speller and enjoys something like that. But I don't know, we've never done anything like that before. I wouldn't be a bit surprised if some of the parents would object.

For Martha's sake, I hope she can have her spelling bee. Since Marc is also boarding at Rudy's now, Martha isn't here much in the evening anymore. She says she goes over to study and take language lessons, but I know that the chief attraction is Marc himself. What about her firm resolution to not get married before she's twenty-five? I'll have to ask her about that.

The week since Marc entered the picture, we haven't noticed any more food or milk missing. Could he have been hiding in the barn? I can't think of any reason Marc would have had to hide.

Maybe it was just a traveler or drifter. We don't see tramps around anymore since the days of welfare checks, but sometimes there are drifters passing through. Maybe we'll never know who it was.

There's a cold northeast wind tonight, and the windmill is clanging away. At least the kitchen is warm and cozy, and the children are gathered around the table getting an early start on making valentines. Red hearts and lace and I Love You's got Martha interested, too. She joined them and made a big valentine for Marc.

Little Crist asked her, "Aren't you going to make one for Melvin, too?"

"Oh sure I am," Martha replied. "I like him, too."

Apparently *like* and *love* aren't the same thing. I'm worried about Martha. Is "love at first sight" a reliable thing to base a relationship on? It's all beyond me. ▦

February 12

*T*onight was the spelling bee. To my surprise, many of the parents were present. No one expressed any opposition. Martha invited Pam and

Gloria and George, and even a few *Schtedtler* (town people) were there.

Martha and Melvin had hung up gas lanterns from the ceiling. Since it was an unseasonably mild evening, a few of the windows were opened, and a soft springlike breeze blew in. I felt a little like I used to feel when I was *rumschpringing* (going out with the youth) and went to a singing!

None of the women had enough spunk to go up front and spell (except Martha, of course), but most of the men did. Just before the spelling began, Rudy came and offered to pronounce the words for the spellers, so Melvin went up to spell, too.

At first the words were easy. Nate was the first to go down. He was given *pumpkin* and spelled it *p-u-n-k-i-n.* Everyone laughed. I know he knew better than that, but *so geht's* (so it goes).

One after another, the others dropped out until all the married men were down. That made the *Yunge* (youth) clap and cheer. Rudy commented dryly that marriage must be hard on one's ability to spell.

Finally the only ones left were Martha, Marc, and Melvin. The words got harder. Then Martha went down on a fairly easy word, *silhouette,* and made a face in disappointment. She was as bad as Nate; she knew how to spell it but simply forgot the silent *h.*

Then the match was between Melvin and Marc. By then everybody was sitting on the edges of their seats and cheering them on.

"Come on, Marc!" Martha called. "Show your stuff. Show Melvin that he isn't the only one with brains."

Melvin's sister Esther cheered for him, calling out encouragement. Back and forth the turns went, and everyone was tense as the words got harder and harder. Rudy could hardly figure out how to pronounce them.

Melvin got the word *phytopathology*, and everyone seemed to hold their breaths until he had it spelled correctly.

Then Marc got *pneumoconiosis*. Surely he wouldn't be able to spell a word like that! But he did, and a ripple of admiration filled the room.

All eyes were on Melvin's face next. So no one noticed that the side door opened and Henry came striding in—until he spoke.

"Here you sit," he scolded with intensity and blazing eyes, "being entertained by a spelling match. What would your ancestors, the Anabaptists, have thought of this? They gathered in caves and cellars, in the dark of night, to have worship services without being discovered by the authorities. And you, *you* sit here being entertained."

Henry's voice was rising as he went on preaching at us: "To be spiritually minded is life and peace, and to be carnally minded is death." Meanwhile folks hurriedly began to get their wraps and leave.

Poor Martha! She had baked lots of cookies and made gallons of drink for refreshments after the spelling bee, but she never got to serve them.

We were a sober, thoughtful group as we walked home with millions of stars twinkling overhead. All except Martha; she was filled with "righteous indignation," as she called it. "How dare he judge us like that!" she sputtered. "He's radical! He's a fanatic! I wish he'd go to Africa if that's what he wants to do."

Ach mei! (oh my), I never once thought that Henry

would make trouble about a spelling bee. My, how he has changed! And Priscilla, too. I remember well when she was a young girl, and I thought she was so shallow and flippant that she would never grow up. I thought she was a *scheene Schissel mit nix drin* (pretty dish with nothing in it).

However, now I know that was only my self-righteous judgment. I thought she wasn't good enough for Isaac, who now is a minister for one of our congregations in Minnesota. Well, I'm glad I was wrong about Priscilla. I just hope that now she and Henry don't become so radical that they become unbalanced.

For Dora's sake especially—sometimes I lie awake at night worrying about Dora. What will become of her there in that faraway land? Sometimes I think that seeing her go will be the hardest thing I've ever gone through—even harder than parting with Amanda.

I try to cling to the promise: "My grace is sufficient for you." But trusting and believing sometimes is uphill work instead of being joyful submission. Many a time I feel like taking to my bed and weeping an ocean of tears. Oh God, undertake for me! ▦

February 13

*R*udy brought Barbianne over this afternoon—her first outing with Baby James. He's one month old today and getting chubbier and cuter every day. *Die Botschaft* (newspaper) came in the mail while they were here. While scanning through it, Barbianne discovered a poem that she thought was absolutely adorable. It is, too, and I'll copy it here:

Where Did You Come From?

Where did you come from, baby dear?
Out of the everywhere into the here.
Where did you get your eyes so blue?
Out of the sky as I came through.

What makes the light in them sparkle and spin?
Some of the starry spikes left in.
Where did you get that little tear?
I found it waiting when I got here.

What makes your forehead so smooth and high?
A soft hand stroked it as I went by.
What makes your cheek like a warm white rose?
Something better than anyone knows.

Whence that three-cornered smile of bliss?
Three angels gave me at once a kiss.
Where did you get that pearly ear?
God spoke and it came out to hear.

Where did you get those arms and hands?
Love made itself into hooks and bands.
Feet, whence did you come, you darling things?
From the same box as the cherubs' wings.

How did they all just come to be you?
God thought about me, and so I grew.
But how did you come to us, you dear?
God thought of you, and so I am here.

—*George Macdonald*

They feel themselves wondrously blessed indeed with their precious little bundle, a gift from heaven. It does my heart good to see them doting over him. Grandpa Daves stopped in while they were here, and Grandma Annie frowned when she saw their devotion to the baby.

"Tsk tsk," she said, shaking her head disapprovingly. "You'll be spoiling that little one yet if you aren't careful."

But Barbianne laughed gaily. "*Ach*, no, Grammie, babies can't be spoiled before they're a year old. That's what babies are for, to love and to cuddle."

Annie shook her head. "Remember that he has a soul to teach, train, and bring up in the nurture and admonishment of the Lord. While he is small, he is pliable and teachable. But once he is grown, he will no longer be as clay in your hands."

"I know," Barbianne said, sobering a bit. "But disciplining and training seem far off yet. We want to do our best when the time comes. But for now, all we have to do in that line is to love and enjoy him."

One thing is sure: that baby will never lack for tender loving care with Barbianne and Rudy as parents! ▓

February 16

*H*enry and Priscilla are bringing the little girls here nearly every day while they go to a training school. I didn't ask for details, and they didn't offer any. But I do know that they are preparing to be missionaries.

Dora comes here after school, and it almost seems like old times again. She is so helpful and good with the children and so friendly and likable that I have to fight my battles all over again. Sometimes I think it just can't be allowed that she goes with them!

Would it do any good to have another talk with Henry and Priscilla to try to persuade them to let Dora stay with us? Nate doesn't think it would, but he has agreed to try. Somehow I just don't feel that it's God's will for her to go to Africa. Maybe we won't have to give her up after all.

I guess I never really did accept the fact that she's going. But maybe—just maybe—she won't go. I keep harboring the thought that perhaps God is testing us to see if we are willing to give her up. Then, like Abraham in the Bible when he was ready to offer up Isaac, God will intervene.

To sum it up, I guess I want to be willing to give up my will, but I don't want to give up Dora. I feel like I'm in a strait betwixt two, torn apart.

Martha seems to be bubbling over with all kinds of good feelings these days—like a beam of sunshine in our home. I like to think that God sent her to us just when we needed her most. ❖

March 8

Springlike weather has arrived early this year. We're having a warm, balmy week.

Maybe if I'd known what Martha is so happy about, I wouldn't have written what I did in my last journal entry. She's out horseback riding with Marc nearly every evening. As soon as supper's over, he comes here, and off they go, over the hills and away.

I'm worried about Martha. When I warn her not to be

too impulsive, or to watch out or she will break her heart, she laughs and says that everything will work out all right. She's apparently living for today and not worrying about tomorrow!

I found out that Martha is not as afraid of mice as Pam is. The cold winter weather had brought an invasion of mice into our house. We're still setting traps for them and catching some at night, but it hasn't seemed to make a dent in their population yet. With spring coming, maybe they'll move out.

This morning when Martha opened the pantry door to get fixings to pack her lunch, she yelled, "There goes a mouse!"

She grabbed a broom, and the chase was on. The mouse ran from the pantry to the *Kellerhals* (cellarway), next to the enclosed porch, and then under the settee. Martha was chasing it and jabbing at it as she went.

Soon she had a broken broom and then happened to punch a hole in the wall plaster. All the while the children were cheering and hollering for her to hit the mouse.

I collapsed weakly into a chair, laughing helplessly, and the mouse got away, much to Martha's disappointment. I consoled her, saying that the mouse had probably been so frightened that he had dropped dead of a heart attack. *So geht's!* (so it goes). ▓

March 12

*P*eter said tonight, "Only two more months, then school's out."

Can it really be possible? My, this term flew as if on

wings! It seems almost too good to be true to have such a good teacher and to have everything go so smoothly.

The children love school so much that they rush through their chores in the morning to get there early. Teacher Melvin makes it so interesting for them that they are enthusiastic about their lessons.

Melvin decided to have a spring program this year instead of a Christmas program, so that's coming up in a few weeks. It wonders me so how Little Crist will do. He has a poem to recite, and I'm hoping he won't forget his lines when he's standing up front.

Yesterday the pupils had a fruit roll for Teacher Melvin. They each took pieces of fruit along to school and hid them in their desks. At nine o'clock (the agreed-on time), two of the upper-grade boys suddenly whistled shrilly together. Teacher Melvin looked up, startled and angry and ready to reprimand them. Then all of a sudden, apples, oranges, grapefruits, tangerines, and even tin cans came rolling up the aisle toward him from each desk. Peter said tonight that Melvin nearly fell over, he was so surprised. He gathered enough fruit to fill a big box to take home.

That was a small way for the children to show their appreciation for the teacher and add some spice to the day. After Franie we are truly grateful to have a teacher like Melvin. Let's hope he won't get married soon and quit teaching, as is the custom, to make a living for his family on the farm. That way his children will have chores to do so they can learn to work.

I am not sorry, though, that Franie boarded with us last winter. I treasure the friendship I have with her now. We exchange letters regularly and visit back and forth occasionally. ❈

Old Man Winter isn't quite done with us yet, but we hope this will be his last fling. After those few days of springlike weather, he came back. Now the wind is whistling around the corners of the house. We had some snow flurries off and on.

Tonight I helped in the barn. As I hurried to the house in the frigid blast, the light from the kitchen windows shone out in welcoming beams, promising warmth and a good supper ready.

Marc must have found it welcoming, too, for he stopped in to warm himself by our kitchen fire on his way home. We invited him to stay for supper.

I hope our neighborhood will always stay as friendly and welcoming as it is now, with everyone treating each other with proper respect. We take time to discuss such things as the weather, the school, the church, the crops, and even government matters.

Marc keeps us informed about what's going on in Washington, and sometimes it doesn't sound too good. Let us remember to pray earnestly for the rulers of our country and our government every day, so that we will be able to continue to lead quiet and peaceable lives and have freedom of religion.

God has set the rulers in place, and we want to obey their laws except when they conflict with God's laws. Our preachers remind us that the government is worldly, using force to punish evildoers. That is so different from Christ's heavenly kingdom of love and forgiveness, to which we belong. ❈

March 26

Melvin was here tonight af-
ter school to help Nate dehorn cattle—a job I slip out of
whenever I can. I don't like to hear them bawling and

struggling. But Peter, Sadie and Crist sat on hay bales to watch, with gruesome delight, while I finished the chores.

Usually the barn is a pleasant place of warmth and life. The cows are softly mooing and eager for their supper, impatient at the sound of the milk pails rattling. Then they contentedly chew their grain and silage.

Old Tabby, the cat, sits close by, waiting for her saucer of milk. The horses stamp their feet and whinny a soft throaty whinny that Martha claims sounds exactly like they are chuckling. The banties roost up in the rafters and say goodnight in a murmuring way.

A mouse scampers by and is gone with a rustling of hay, but Tiger, our best mouser, is after it in a flash, standing guard at the mouse hole, licking his whiskers and waving his tail. Next we'll have to bring him into the house to catch the mice.

When the animals are all fed and bedded down for the night, all is quiet and peaceful except for the muted animal sounds. The barn is a pleasant place to be—but not when the dehorning is being done! I headed for the house as soon as I could. I'm always glad when that job is done for another year. Then we know the cattle won't be gouging each other—or us! ✳

April 3

Springtime is here to stay at last! This morning at dawn I heard a robin joyously singing, and I wondered if there are any robins in Africa. What is spring like there? Do they have tulips, daffodils, and hyacinths?

I had Dora, Priscilla, Henry, and the little girls so much in my thoughts this morning that I went to the phone shanty and dialed their number. The phone rang for a long time, then Henry answered.

"The mission board wants us to leave in a few days," he said, almost breathlessly. "We have our passports and visas, and everything has finally gone through."

"In a few days!" I cried in dismay. "Couldn't you come over for dinner one more time before you go?"

Henry studied a bit, then said he thinks they could come today. We were all overjoyed and quickly tidied up the house. Since it was Saturday, Martha and the children were home, too.

I had already made plans to plant the garden, so Martha offered to prepare the dinner, with Sadie's help. Peter and Crist helped me drop the seeds into the neat furrows and cover them with rich, dark soil. For some reason I felt more lighthearted and joyous than I had for a long time. I just felt in my bones that perhaps I could still persuade Dora to stay with us.

So I worked happily with the boys, planting peas, potatoes, onions, cabbage, lettuce, parsley, and red beets. Meanwhile, the song sparrows and robins sang with joyous abandon. Peter and Crist each wanted a little garden of their own, so I helped them plan that. Then we planted a row of bright-faced pansies along the edge of the garden.

While we were washing our hands at the pump, Henrys drove in, and I hurried into the house, confident that Martha would have a good dinner ready. She did! Every room of the house was filled with the wonderful aroma of freshly baked biscuits, roast beef, gravy, mashed potatoes, and scalloped corn.

I welcomed Priscilla warmly, trying not to think of their leaving. I had a wild, unreasonable hope that surely something would happen yet to prevent them from leaving.

We put chairs and benches around the kitchen, set the food on the table, and served the meal cafeteria style. That way Henry and Priscilla wouldn't have to sit by themselves at the little table.

It was a day of precious memories, a cherished visit. I held little Bathsheba as long as she allowed it and tried to form an unforgettable picture in my mind of her and Miriam Joy to put into my memories chest.

Priscilla talked of how eager she and Henry are to go.

I asked, "Is Dora eager to go to Africa, too?"

Priscilla quickly replied, a trifle sharply, "Of course she wants to go along."

I tried to put the thought of their leaving out of my mind and enjoy the day to the fullest. It was an enjoyable day until just before they were ready to leave. Then I made the mistake of impulsively throwing my arms around Dora and asking, "Which would you rather do, go along or stay with us?"

Dora burst into tears. ⌗

April 17

*W*hen Nate's biopsy came back negative last year, I was so happy that life seemed like a joyous thing, full and satisfying. But now since Dora has really gone, life seems to have lost its flavor.

Before she actually left, I still had the underlying hope, however groundless, that she wouldn't go along after all.

But now that we are separated by the ocean wide, it seems so final. Oh, my precious daughter, how could she have left us like that?

Martha is like a sunbeam of cheer in our home. I often wonder, did God really send her to us because he knew we needed cheering up? Since spring is here, she and Marc are together more than ever, horseback riding, hiking, and going for bicycle rides. She comes back in, her face aglow, raving over the beauties of the countryside in springtime.

Sometimes I envy her and wistfully think back to the evening drives I used to take with Nate. Life was so carefree then, or does it just seem that way to me now?

Nevertheless, tonight Martha came home in tears, after a jaunt in the city with Marc. Melvin had just brought the church bench wagon (we're having church here a week from tomorrow), so he heard her story, too. She plopped down on the grass beside the wagon while I helped Melvin unhitch the horses.

"I wish I'd never have gone to that stupid fortune-teller!" Martha cried petulantly with a toss of her blond ponytail. "It makes me so mad."

"What!" Melvin exclaimed, sounding alarmed. "You didn't really go to a fortune-teller, did you?"

"Yes, we did," Martha said disgustedly, "and it cost us thirty-five dollars apiece, too, all for listening to a bunch of lies."

"But not all fortune-telling is lies," Melvin soberly declared. "Sometimes they really do have occult powers to discern the future."

"Well, this one didn't," Martha said indignantly. "She told me that I would go to a foreign country and marry a dark-skinned native. Imagine that! And she told Marc that he has sorrow ahead of him! I'm sure of one thing, I'll never go to a fortune-teller again."

Nate came into the barnyard just then with the horses and sulky plow, after a day of plowing, and heard the story, too.

"You did a foolish thing," he told Martha. "Going to a fortune-teller is dangerous. What if she would have hypnotized you? We can't have God's protection if we fool around with the occult. You can thank God that you came out of it safe and sound."

By this time, Martha was thoroughly frightened.

"Let me tell you what happened to my dad," Nate told her. "Over seventy years ago, a group of wandering horse traders were camping right here in this very meadow." He motioned toward the creek valley.

"One of them came to the house and bamboozled Dad into trading one of his best horses for an old broken-down hag, and into giving all the money he had in the house along with it yet, in the bargain. I've heard that if they can get you to say *yes*, they have you."

Martha shivered. "It sounds awful," she responded weakly. "I had no idea. We just wanted to have a bit of fun. But I learned my lesson. I'll just try to forget what he said and trust God to lead and direct my life."

I was glad to hear her say that, for she has never before really made a profession of faith. We've grown fond of Martha and want the best for her. ▓

*I*t feels so good to sit down
and rest my weary feet tonight. We had a busy day of getting ready for church here tomorrow, and now I think I
can say we're actually ready. The house is spick-and-span,
the folding doors are opened, and the benches are all set
in place.

Rudy and Barbianne were here to help, also Grandpa
Daves and the families of neighbors Eli and Emanuel. The
Schnitzboi (dried-apple pies) are all made and waiting on
the pantry shelves. The church spread (a combination of
peanut butter and molasses) is mixed, and the washhouse
table is filled with loaves of freshly baked brown bread.

Crocks of smearcase (cottage cheese) are ready. Cans
of red beets and pickles are on the shelf, and the dried
meadow tea from last summer is waiting to be brewed. As
usual, it will be a quick and simple meal.

We are having *Grossgmee* (communion) tomorrow, so
the services will last well into the afternoon. Martha has
been attending our church services faithfully and wearing
her Amish clothes on Sundays, "just for the fun of it," she
says. She has no plans to become a member. So, since
Grossgmee is only for the members, she will stay at Pam's
with Peter, Sadie, and Crist tomorrow.

Martha is seriously studying Marc's religion but has not
committed herself to anything yet. We are concerned and
will continue to pray for her.

Now I want to study the fourth part of Thomas à
Kempis's *The Imitation of Christ*. It is entitled "A Devout
Exhortation to the Holy Communion." This will help to
prepare my soul for the Lord's Supper tomorrow.

Actually, the last half year should have been a daily preparation, but there is still time to search the soul and repent of all known sin, time to lay aside the weights which so easily beset us on our spiritual journey heavenward. ▦

*T*he last day of school. We had our annual end-of-the-year school picnic for the parents and school-age and preschool children. Each family brought a hot covered dish and a cold one.

Since we had too much to carry with my big roast pan of scalloped potatoes, Nate hitched the workhorses to the wagon. The children clambered happily on back, and we started off.

The morning was beautiful and cool, with bobwhites calling from the meadows and the sweet fragrance of dewy clover fields wafting on the breeze. The horses stepped lively, their heavy rumps bouncing up and down. The fields and meadows were lush and green, dotted with myriads of buttercups.

It would have been a wonderful day if my heart had not been aching for Dora. Why haven't we heard from her yet? They've been gone for nearly six weeks now. Priscilla has written a few short notes in reply to our letters, but nothing specifically about Dora.

Is she happy there, so happy that she never thinks about us anymore? Where did she finish her school term? I wish Priscilla would see to it that Dora writes to us, or at least give us news of Dora in her own letters.

I think I'll write another letter to both Priscilla and

Dora tonight and urge their reply. I can't stand not knowing how Dora is adjusting. It's entirely too much for a mother-heart to bear! ✳

*A*pple-blossom time is here again. What a lovely time of year! Sadie and I went for a walk tonight in the lower meadow. It was such a warm spring night that I thought any minute the fireflies would come out, but it's too early for that.

Bushytail, the gray squirrel, watched us from his perch in the pine tree, suspicious of us. He ran up and down the tree cocking his head this way and that and swishing his tail, scolding and chattering at us for invading his area.

It was heavenly walking under the old Maiden Blush apple tree, sucking in deep breaths of the delicate and exquisite perfume of the falling blossoms. Sadie's eyes danced with awe and gladness. I knew that all the beauty wasn't lost on her. Hand in hand we traipsed homeward, our hearts too full for words.

The cows, lowing softly, came down the cow lane, contented and peaceful after being relieved of their burdens of milk. The chickens were clucking in the barnyard, and then flew up into the trees to roost.

I was reminded of the song "Peace Overflowing." If only I could feel at peace about Dora. I have an unhappy premonition that all is not well with her, but, oh! how I hope I'm wrong! I remind myself that God can take care of Dora across the ocean the same as he could here. That makes me feel somewhat better. ✳

May 21

Martha has left with Marc on a trip to Colorado to meet his parents and to learn more about his religious beliefs. Already I miss her; it seems like a cloud is blocking the sunbeams, throwing a shadow over us.

Before she left, she told me, "I mean to make a definite decision before I come back. Marc wants me to marry him, but he will not change his beliefs or give them up. I've been living in limbo these last weeks, and the time has come for me to make up my mind."

She swallowed hard, and I could tell that the decision would not be easy for her. I've felt a burden for her ever since, realizing how easy it is for young people to be blinded by love.

However, I believe she knows it is difficult enough to make a go of marriage even when both partners think alike about the most important thing of all—their religious beliefs. What would it be like to try to raise a family if the mother and father were of different faiths?

Tonight we mowed the yard for the second time. Peter and Sadie were pulling at the clattering push mower like two workhorses with ropes around their middles, and I was pushing and steering. We had good family fun while we got the job done.

The lilacs are blooming, wafting their sweet fragrance on the evening air.

I feel homesick tonight, for Dora and Amanda and Martha. My thoughts stray to that glad place over yonder where no one will ever need to say goodbye. ❄

*W*ell, Martha and Marc are back, but neither of them seemed happy as they came in the door together. She welcomed the children crowding around her with a forced cheerfulness. Then after they had run off to play, she sat on the settee with her legs crossed beneath her and spoke to Marc, Nate, and me about what lay heavy on her heart.

"I've done everything they asked me to do," she stated listlessly. "I prayed, I fasted, I visited the temple and talked with other missionaries. The more I learned, the more sure I am that I can never believe like you do, Marc."

She broke down and sobbed, and Marc cried with her.

"I can't marry you if we don't believe alike," she cried brokenly. "So this must be the end of our friendship."

Marc shook his head helplessly. "I—I can't change," he said sadly. "I have to be true to my convictions. It's like a wall—the family traditions and beliefs from generations past. And I have to be true to them.

"If this is the end, then I'll have to be leaving. I'll pick up my things at Rudy's and move back to the city. I couldn't bear to stay here."

Martha was crying quietly, and my heart ached for them both. But no one could think of any other way out of their dilemma. So Marc left, and Martha retreated to her room.

"She should have thought of that before she fell for him," Nate said in a matter-of-fact tone of voice. "She only caused a lot of heartache for them both. But there's nothing on earth that heaven can't heal, with time."

I nodded wordlessly. Martha is still young, too young

to be thinking of getting married anyway. But I feel, oh, so sorry, for both of them. ▦

*A*t last today I had a letter from Priscilla that was more than a note. I tore open the envelope with trembling fingers.

She wrote, "Dora is suffering from what they call 'culture shock.' She's having a hard time making herself at home here and has been rather homesick. We feel that things will soon go a lot better for her, but it will take time.

"She has written letters to you, but I didn't send them, for I kept thinking that by the time you'd have received them, things would already be going a lot better. I didn't want you to feel bad."

I threw the letter down and stormed about the house, having to let off steam some way. I was angry at both Henry and Priscilla for taking Dora along, and angry at myself for having allowed it.

Oh, how I ached to have Dora back here with us. If only I could somehow talk to her on the telephone. I wonder, do telephone lines cross the ocean?

However, there's not a thing I could do anyway, with so many miles between us. I wonder if there is anything harder than being separated from one of your children when they are hurting or in trouble. ▦

*T*onight Crist and I went to bring up a few straggling cows from the lower meadow. The soothing peacefulness of the lovely, misty meadowlands calmed my ruffled spirits.

Wild cherry trees were in blossom, and the air was wonderfully fragrant and sweet smelling. A robin sang sweetly and joyously from somewhere high up among the blossoms. The grass was lush and green beside the cow path. A few late buttercups lifted their bit of sunshine to the skies.

I wondered, Are there lovely meadows and brooks, trees and butterflies, songbirds and flowers in Africa, to cheer Dora's heart? Is it springtime there, too? Oh Dora, I thought, there is an ache in my heart that won't go away until you, too, are here walking along the cow path in the meadow with us.

Crist was chattering brightly, hopping and skipping about, excited to be going barefooted for the first time this spring. He's a comfort to me, as are the other children.

I have to think of the Amish couple whose little eighteen-month-old son was killed last week when the milk truck backed over him. At least they know that he is safe in the arms of Jesus, not in some faraway country, suffering who knows what. But I feel guilty having such thoughts, for I know that Priscilla needs Dora there.

Oh God, help us all! ✵

*T*he back porch is a pleasant place in June. At one end is the huge old honeysuckle vine just loaded with the sweetest smelling blossoms. Climbing the lattice at the other end are lovely, fragrant old-fashioned red rambler roses. Both are a haven for birds and honeybees.

We all sat on the porch tonight after our day's work, enjoying the coolness and fragrance of the evening after a busy day with strawberries and haymaking. Melvin stayed to help as *Gnecht* (hired man) at Rudy's over the summer. Today they both helped Nate with haymaking here on the farm.

Tonight Barbianne came over, too, pushing little James in the stroller. We gathered on the porch for a real visit once again.

Martha joined us, but the old exuberance and animation are no longer there. How I would love to see the old twinkle in her eyes once again, and her bubbling joy and wry sense of humor. Between her and my worries about Dora, we can both be rather glum these days.

Baby James cheered up all of us with his cooing and gurgles and bright smiles. He's such a dear, cute, lovable chap. What would this world be without babies and toddlers? Childhood joy and laughter is so contagious and pure that it tugs at one's heartstrings.

This reminds me of a verse I once heard: "A dreary place would be this earth, were there no little people in it." And I feel a twinge of sadness that my own "babies" are growing up so fast. ❖

*G*loria Graham was here to-night. It was good to have something else to think about besides Dora's homesickness and Martha's troubles. She brought along Itsy Bitsy, her Pomeranian puppy, and cooed so much baby talk to him that it was almost embarrassing. If she doesn't kiss him, it comes awfully close to it.

When the doggie went to sleep on her lap, Gloria reported on something that upset her quite a bit. She stopped at an Amish farmer's roadside stand today and bought a quart box of late strawberries. The berries on the top were big and luscious looking. But when she began to cap them, she found that only the top layer of berries were big; the rest were small and not very nice.

Well! I can't blame her for being unhappy about it. I told her that the farmers usually have their children helping with the berries, and maybe an innocent child did it.

However, Gloria snorted at that. "A child wouldn't have done that unless Papa instructed him to! When I pass that way again, I'm going to stop and give him a piece of my mind. I'll demand a refund of my money, too. He's not getting away with that, the rascal!"

Oh dear! Well, I just hope she won't judge them all by him. Just what would she think if she knew about what happened here in Pennsylvania, about two hundred years ago. Henry Yoder, a young Amish man living in another county, was interested in a girl named Barbara Lehman, but she did not accept his offer of friendship.

One spring evening he decided to go to see her and try once more to win her. She boarded with her brother-in-law and sister, John and Magdalene Hochstetler. Before he got to the house, he saw Barbara and her sister Magdalene hurry from the house to the sugar camp nearby. They were unaware of his presence, but he thought they were hurrying off to get away from him.

He knew that John and Magdalene were opposed to having him court Barbara. In his heartache and anger, he wanted to hurt them back somehow. When the women were out of sight, he sneaked into the house, probably merely intending to damage some of their property. But there lay six-month-old baby Susanna, peacefully sleeping in her cradle.

This Henry Yoder likely intended to give the parents a scare by hiding the baby, but the plan went awry. He put baby Susanna into the small trundle bed in the bedroom and shoved it under the big bed. When the baby's parents and Barbara returned to the house shortly afterward, imagine their anguish at finding the baby gone and then later finding her smothered to death under the mattress!

John hurried to the neighbors to report the tragedy, while Magdalene and Barbara waited alone in the house. Suddenly Barbara was startled to see a man looking in the window, and fearfully she grabbed a log by the fireplace. Then the mysterious figure was gone.

When asked who she thought it might have been, Barbara named John's brother Solomon, because the man had worn a colorful hunting shirt like Solomon's. John and Magdalene, although they had no proof, chose to believe that Solomon was the mischief-maker whose deed brought death.

Feelings were not good between the two brothers at the time. They already were not on speaking terms with each other. From then on until his death, half a century later, John falsely blamed Solomon for killing his daughter and would have nothing to do with him.

Others shunned Solomon too, and he began drinking to forget about his troubles. Several years after John died, Henry Yoder, on what he thought was his deathbed, confessed that he was responsible for Susanna being smothered fifty years earlier.

Solomon broke down and cried when he heard the news. At long last he was free of his burden of being falsely accused. How he regretted that his brother John was no longer living so they could be reconciled. He had, in his old age, finally renewed his faith and relationship with God and the church. One can hardly blame him for being brokenhearted and bitter during the years of shunning and injustice. It's a sad, sad story.

That also somehow reminds me of the story of Yonie Kauffman, a young Amish boy who was *rumschpringing* (running around with the youth) in the early 1900s. Yonie was dating a girl named Mary Stoltzfus, and he thought a lot of her. But for some reason he was not sure of her friendship.

Each Sunday evening before he left for home, he asked her if he could come back. He trembled in his shoes, afraid that her answer this time would be no.

One evening the young folks had a cornhusking planned. When Yonie arrived, groups of boys and girls were already gathered around each shock, husking the golden ears amid much good-natured visiting and laughter.

Yonie passed each group until he found the one he was looking for. "Good evening, Mary," he said shyly. Mary returned his greeting, but just then another boy walked over to greet Mary, too, and she gave him a warm smile.

Yonie's heart surged with jealousy. As the evening wore on, the young folks changed partners, and Yonie found himself with a group of boys only. One of them had brought a jug of hard cider, which was passed around.

"Come on, Yonie," one called to him. "You worked harder than the rest of us, and you have a long ride home."

The other boys urged him on, too. Yonie was reluctant, but finally he took a swallow. The jug was passed again, and the boys urged him to drink more. He did.

This went on until he began to feel a bit dizzy and light-headed. Suddenly he realized what the boys were doing by the gleam of mischief in their eyes. He sensed a plot, and he stalked away in disgust and anger. How foolish he had been! If only he had never taken that first swallow.

He knew how Mary felt about strong drink, and if she found out, as she was sure to do, their friendship would come to an abrupt end. There was little doubt in his mind and little hope in his heart.

As it turned out, Yonie's fears were not unfounded. Mary Stoltzfus was sorry but convinced that their friendship should end. She had another way home from the singings after that—with the boy who had greeted her by the corn shock, to whom she had given the warm smile. Yonie was convinced that this same boy had started the plotting with the jug. He was devastated.

To escape the unpleasant memories, he left for an Amish community in another county. Several weeks later his parents received a letter from that community stating that Yonie had left that area, without saying where he was going. They had no idea where he had gone.

Yonie's parents wept when they heard the news that Yonie had gone. They prayed and eagerly watched the mailbox for a letter from him, but none came. For twenty-nine years Yonie lived the life of a wandering sailor, drinking, gambling, and bumming around the world. Then finally he came to his senses.

One Sunday morning found him walking in the lane at his parents former home, not knowing that both his parents had been dead for eight or nine years already. No one was home. At another farm, though, he met an Amish acquaintance who hitched up his horse and buggy and alerted Yonie's brothers and sisters that their long-lost brother had returned.

They welcomed him warmly and forgave him. Yonie was a changed man. He repented and was sorry for the pain and sadness he had caused his family by his disappearance. Yonie wanted to live a better life. He sought God's forgiveness and prayed for mercy for his soul.

This is a sad story of a life wasted in sin, but it has a happier ending. I'm sure that the boys who had a part in Yonie's downfall also suffered much from remorse and guilty consciences. There is a lesson in it for us, especially for the young folks of today. ❀

June 30

*M*artha's naturally bubbly personality seems to be helping her during this down time in her life. She's gradually bouncing back. Martha spends most of her spare time in the barn with the animals or out horseback riding alone.

Last night she told me, "I feel perfectly at home in your dear old cobwebby barn. I even like to climb into the hay-mow, peek out the little window, and look out over the fields, woods, and meadows, and the winding creek and the hills. I think if I ever get over missing Marc, I'll try to fall in love with a farmer next time."

She giggled then, and I knew she was well on the way to recovery, to having her heart mended.

Martha went on, "There's just something peaceful and soothing in the atmosphere of an old-fashioned barn. The horses whinny a throaty welcome to me, and I like to pat their velvety noses. The cows aren't quite as affectionate, but I think their soft moos mean that they like me, too. And the barn cats swarm around me like bees to a honey pot. It helps to satisfy a wounded ego."

"Wounded ego?" I repeated. "Do you mean that you thought Marc would leave his church for you?"

Martha shrugged her shoulders, then said wistfully, "It would've been nice to be loved that much, don't you think? But then, I couldn't expect him to do what I wasn't able to do, could I?"

She had answered her own question, so to speak. She brightened noticeably when she realized that Marc had to put first his love for God and faithfulness to his beliefs as he understood them—no matter how much he loved her. I expect Marc felt somewhat rejected too, at first, just as she did.

Well, time is a great healer, and they are still young. Maybe in a few years from now, they'll look back and thank God for this experience. ▦

*P*amela came to the door this afternoon and hurried in without knocking. "Come quick," she gasped, almost out of breath. "Priscilla telephoned from Africa and told me to come and get you. She'll call back again in a few minutes."

I think I was in shock, for I couldn't move right away. Calling from Africa! Was such a thing really possible? I felt like I was glued to the floor.

Finally Nate had to tell me to hurry up and go with Pam so I wouldn't miss Priscilla's call. I moved then, and a short time later I was hearing Priscilla's quavering voice on the line. "We're just about at wit's end. We don't know what to do about Dora. She just won't get over being homesick.

"She doesn't eat much, and she's getting thin and hollow eyed. We kept thinking she'd soon get over it, but it's getting worse instead of better. She doesn't take an interest in anything here and just keeps saying she wants to go home. What shall we do?"

Without thinking, I replied, "Oh please, bring her home right away. I can't bear it; she must come home!" My voice and my thoughts weren't very rational.

"We would if we could," Priscilla said sadly. "But it's just not possible." Then she added in a small voice, "We should have left her with you. . . . Couldn't you come and take her home?"

"Me?" I exclaimed in astonishment. "I wouldn't know the way."

Priscilla chuckled in spite of herself. "Not just you, but someone from there. Do you think Pam could come and take her back there? Maybe the church people would pay her traveling expenses. Talk it over and call me back again in a few hours."

She gave her telephone number and hung up. As soon as the receiver was down, I wished so much I would have asked to talk with Dora. But my thoughts were in such a whirl that I was dazed and couldn't think straight.

Pam took me home, and we talked things over. She told us it wasn't possible for her to make the trip. Pam suggested that we ask Gloria and George, since they are experienced travelers.

Nate decided that he would call back and talk with Dora, encouraging her to try to buck up and make the best of things until Henry and Priscilla come back on furlough.

So we both talked to Dora. But she just sobbed the whole time. It was so heartrending. Nate talked with Henry, then again with Dora, and he got real stern with her and told her that she would have to stop acting like a baby.

I thought it was unbearably cruel and heartless, and I wanted to stop him, but instead I just sat there and cried. Oh, what a helpless feeling!

I thought of the words of a hymn, "Does Jesus care, when my heart is pained, too deeply for word or for song? When my sad heart aches, till it nearly breaks, Is it ought to him? Does he care?" I know the answer, but I can't feel it just now. God seems so far away. ❋

July 5

*A*s soon as Teacher Melvin heard about our dilemma, he offered right away to go to Africa and bring Dora home. In fact, he was delighted to have an excuse to travel.

Then when Martha came home from work and heard the story, she declared that she was going with Melvin. "I need a change badly, and I want to see Africa, too."

Hurried plans were being made. Then Nate motioned me aside and said, "Surely it wouldn't be proper for a young girl, an outsider, and an Amish boy to go traveling together like that."

I just stared wordlessly at him. Oh, how I wanted Dora to be safely brought back.

When Preacher Emanuel stopped in, Nate asked him about it. He didn't approve of it, either. He said, "The Bible says, 'Abstain from all appearance of evil,' and I think this would come into that category."

So together they confronted Martha and asked her to stay at home. I can guess how she's taking it. She went to her room and closed the door a bit louder than necessary.

Melvin is making the needed arrangements, getting information on the best way to go besides by plane, for that would be against the *Ordnung* (church rules). The ministers say that God didn't create us with wings and doesn't want airships intruding into heaven.

Henry sent a message via Pam this afternoon urging us to please, somehow or other, come and take Dora home. Nate's scolding didn't work its intended purpose. Dora's frighteningly quiet and withdrawn now, and they are getting alarmed about her.

I wish Melvin could get there faster. As soon as Dora knows Melvin is on the way, perhaps she'll cheer up. It's so hard not to be able to do anything for her. At least we can pray. There is comfort in that. ▦

Our hearts are a lot lighter these days since Melvin is in Africa and Dora is feeling a lot better. He is staying as long as he can, not intending to start for home until he must to be back in time for the first day of school.

And guess what! Martha is in Africa too! After Melvin left and she got over her pouting, she up and bought herself a plane ticket with money she'd saved. She went to Africa, too. Martha sure is spunky, there's no doubt about that.

Now we're getting some real newsletters from both of them, and from Dora too. She's happy and excited about coming home with Melvin. I just hope Priscilla won't persuade her to stay after all, now that she's cheered up so much.

Martha wrote that the missionaries there have a lifestyle similar to the Amish in Pennsylvania, without many conveniences. But she wrote, "There in Pa., you can reach for a telephone and have access to immediate medical attention, get a ride, and count on available fuel more easily.

"Here they are in a remote area. They catch rainwater, store it, then use it for dishwashing, cooking, and laundry. Nightly baths consist of a single bucket of rainwater for each of them."

She wrote about animists, who worship spirits in nature, she explained. Many of them view work as the woman's responsibility. Therefore the men spend their time drinking and fighting.

Can they ever be taught to work diligently and live soberly? That it can be pleasurable and rewarding to work hard and faithfully to learn to provide for themselves and their families?

Martha also wrote that some African water is so contaminated that they have to boil it for ten minutes just for it to be fit to rinse a toothbrush in. Wow! Our well water here is too high in nitrates, but at least it's bacteria free. We have to filter it by reverse osmosis process to remove the nitrates. It sure would disgust me to boil all our drinking water and have to drink it lukewarm.

I believe we are somewhat spoiled here in America. Do we realize what a blessing it is to draw a glass of cold, clear, fresh sparkling water right out of the well on a warm summer day, fit and ready to drink?

Martha also wrote that she likes it there and plans to stay for a few months at the least. So it seems as though we've just traded Martha for Dora, at least for awhile. I know that Martha will be a big help to Priscilla and Henry, while Dora was a problem with her *Heemweb* (homesickness).

I can hardly wait to see her again, and I'm counting the days. Melvin wrote about the different foods they have there. There is starfruit, papaya, and mbeli, something like cranberries but sweeter and used to make jelly. Eggs are eighty cents each, and a box of cornflakes costs eight dollars. Whew!

Rice has to be picked over for stones. They have to be careful about chiggers which can get between fingers and toes, and burrow under the skin where they lay eggs. Malaria is not uncommon, but at least they have medication for it.

I've heard it said that half the world doesn't know how

the other half lives, and that has a ring of truth to it. According to an article in the paper that Pam sent over, there are around a hundred fifty thousand Amish people in America. What a small percentage that is compared to the over five and a half billion world population!

Since each billion is a thousand million, and each million is ten hundred thousand, we're just a tiny drop in the bucket, incredibly insignificant by number, a tiny fraction of one percent. Somehow, to me it's a comforting thought. I wonder why? ✳

August 27

*M*elvin and Dora came home today, and what a homecoming it was! The children all crowded around Dora and fired questions at her as fast as they could.

In the midst of it all, I had a disturbing thought. What if Dora gets homesick for Priscilla and Henry? But there doesn't seem to be any danger of that just now.

Dora gazed around with stars in her eyes. "I nearly forgot what you all looked like!" she exclaimed.

She took Sadie and Crist by the hand and walked around the kitchen, taking in everything. "Your kitchen is so big and homey," she declared. "And, mmmm, I smell bread baking! And what's that other good smell coming from the oven? I could eat a table full, I'm so hungry."

Nate came in and fondly tweaked her ear. She gave him a smile that meant complete forgiveness.

Grandpa Dave and Grandma Annie hitched up and drove right over . The twinkle in Dave's old blue eyes and

Annie's beaming face gave Dora a first-rate welcome. It was matched by the gladness in Dora's eyes.

Our family is together again, and the ache in my heart is gone. To think that I, for a while, nearly envied the family that lost their little son. I feel again as if "God's in his heaven; All's right with the world" (R. Browning). But we sure do miss Martha, too. ⚏

August 30

School bells are ringing again, and the children (all four) happily skipped off to school this morning, eager for another year of playing and learning, of lessons and book learning with Teacher Melvin. He has the knack of making book learning interesting.

He tells the pupils, "If you don't read, you don't know. If you don't know, you don't care. If you don't care, you don't succeed. If you don't succeed, you'd better read!"

We are having damp, drizzly, and chilly weather today and yesterday. I have a little fire crackling in the woodstove, whispering that warm and homey message of comfort and taking the chill out of the kitchen. It's an early reminder that fall is on its way.

The house seems empty, but my heart is full, now that Dora is one of us again. I rejoice that once again all four children come traipsing home at lunchtime. They only have half days of school this first week.

When the heart is light, there are a lot of little everyday joys put together that make up the picture of happiness and contentment. Such things as the fragrance of apples drying on the big black range, the sound of a hoot owl at night, and the fragrance of the purple grapes ripening on the vine.

Gray spirals of smoke rising from neighbors' chimneys remind us of their friendship and goodwill and willingness to help in time of need. Pam dropped in to chat for a few minutes. I keep her supplied with things like homemade bread, smearcase, and dried apples because she does so much for us. She's nearly finished with her novel set in Civil War days. I'm eager to read it.

I haven't read many novels yet. After she left, I helped Nate in the barn for awhile. We had time for a heart-to-heart talk once again.

Although he never said much, he had suffered as much as I did when Dora was gone. He said that it seems like one of our missing sunbeams is back. She is one of our golden sunbeams, too, and our family is not complete without her.

Since then, I've been thinking deep thoughts about our little "angel sunbeam" Amanda, shining brightly on heaven's shore. She cannot come back to us, but we can go to her if we are one of God's children. ✤

October 15

We've been hearing a cricket all fall, from somewhere underneath the sideboard. Peter has tried to capture it, but I hope he doesn't succeed. I like to hear his friendly chirping.

Our south field is dotted with corn shocks this year, and the wild geese are winging their way south. The apple trees are loaded with fruit, so we'll have plenty of cider.

We had a pear *schnitzing* (frolic) to make pear butter. It was a warm evening so we sat outside under the grape arbor with only a lantern and the warm glow of the harvest moon for lighting. Grandpa Daves, Rudy and Barbianne, and even Pam came to help.

Everyone seemed to be in a jovial mood. The silos are filled, and cellars are filled with canned goods, and barns and granaries are well stocked for another year. Harvesting is nearly done, and God has again blessed us with plenty to eat and seen us through another season.

My thoughts were with Priscilla, Henry, and Martha, and I selfishly wished them back here with us. We miss them all so much! I'm sure that Dora misses them most of all, but she doesn't complain. She appears happy and contented.

Grandpa Dave told a lot of stories again. I believe he enjoyed it as much as we enjoyed listening to them. His keen blue eyes twinkled merrily when he told a joke.

Little James toddled around on sturdy but unsteady little legs with a devoted Sadie and Crist holding his hand on either side. It won't be long till he's walking on his own at the rate he's going. We all spoil him shamelessly. But he's the only baby we have around to spoil anymore since Henrys are gone, and he's absolutely adorable and irresistible. Oh well, he's not quite a year old yet.

It was another evening for my storehouse of precious memories. Pam said that she cherishes these evenings with us, too, and she claims that she gets a lot of ideas for her book from us. Oh dear, I just hope she doesn't put us in her book!

Today was a most lovely October day with sunshine and bright blue skies, clear and crisp with a sweeping wind—the kind of weather that makes us glad to be alive. We all piled on the spring wagon and drove up the old woods road to gather bushels of hickory nuts and black walnuts.

The horses, with their fat rumps, moved right lively, and we soon were up at the top of the ridge. Squirrels and chipmunks were already busy gathering nuts for the winter, and a few honking geese passed overhead.

There's a magnificent view from up there. We could see all the neighboring farms, the fields looking like a patchwork quilt down in the valley, and the barns and silos full of summer's bounty. The trees along the creek were gorgeous with leaves of vibrant yellow, rich red, and warm gold. The air was mellow and tangy with the scent of decaying leaves and old woodsmoke, and the pungent, indescribable aromas of autumn.

At lunchtime we built a fire to heat our big kettle of vegetable soup. On a tablecloth, we spread our lunch of soup, bologna sandwiches, chowchow, cookies, and a jug of cider. It's not hard to figure out why the meal tastes so much better out in the woodsy autumn splendor, with crinkled brown leaves floating gently down around us. The food took on the flavor of autumn sunshine and scents and breezes.

While gathering firewood, Peter suddenly yelped. He had nearly stepped on a cottontail bunny, which bounded away down the hillside. Sadie gathered colorful leaves and put them in the pocket of her dress, under her *Schatzli* (little apron). Crist played in the pile of leaves.

Meanwhile, Dora sat on a fallen log with her hands clasped around her knees, gazing across the valley with a dreamy, faraway look in her eyes. I wonder, Is she dreaming of Africa?

Nate leaned back against a tree to take a nap, and the mellow sweetness of the autumn sunshine made me sleepy, too. But then a flock of raucous, noisy crows disturbed our peace. Their caw, caw, caws echoed down over the valley. So we got back to work, gathering up our leftovers and filling our baskets.

Later, driving home along the rutted, bumpy lane with the children happily chattering on the back of the spring wagon, I reflected back over the past year. I decided that life seemed full and satisfying once again, after going through what we did when Dora was away. Then too, there's a certain tranquil peace after the harvest, the kind of tired peace one feels after a hard day's work.

All summer we've been working to put away winter food for us and the farm animals, filling the cellar shelves and bins, and in the barn filling haylofts, granaries, and silos. Piles of firewood are neatly stacked in the woodshed.

Peace and plenty, home and hearth—enough to keep the family and the animals fed and warm and comfortable when the winter winds howl and grasp us in their icy grip. Let us with grateful hearts thank the Giver of every good and perfect gift. ▉

*T*here's over a month yet until winter is officially here, but it sure seems like winter already! Last night I awoke to hear sleet rattling noisily against the windowpanes, then sometime during the night the snow came, softly and gently covering every twig, bush, and fencepost.

It was a beautiful sight, and the children were over-joyed to see it when they came shivering downstairs to get dressed in front of the range. This must be what they call squaw winter. Next week we might be having Indian sum-mer again. But I dug out the long johns and the comforters for the beds anyway.

The mail carrier was able to go in spite of the snow. My tramp to the mailbox was well worth it, for I found a letter there! A bubbly, enthusiastic letter from Martha, full of in-teresting bits and pieces of news from Africa.

She is enthusiastic about her newfound friend, Chad Budhram. "He is the kindest, gentlest man I ever met, even more kindhearted than Nate." Well, that sure is a compli-ment!

Martha didn't mention how old he is, so maybe he's a man Grandpa Dave's age. She has the knack for making friends of all ages. I have a feeling she won't be pining for Marc much longer. Maybe she has already forgotten him. She's planning to stay in Africa at least until spring, maybe longer. Then she plans to come back to us again. I'm glad to hear that, for we've all grown fond of her.

Barbianne had a quilting planned for the neighbor-hood women this afternoon. Rudy was kind enough to hitch his horse to the sleigh and drive over for Grandma

Annie and me. It was a lovely ride through the fresh, invigorating air and snowy countryside.

The cold put some roses into our cheeks. Barbianne's kitchen felt warm and cozy as we came in from the frosty outdoors. She had an Irish chain quilt in the frame, a beautiful blue and beige.

Pam was there, and she's every bit as adept at quilting now as the best of them. It gave us all a chance to exchange some news and bits of gossip, and I imagine the tongues flew about as fast as the needles and thimbles. ▓

December 3

*H*og butchering time again. Yesterday Nate sharpened all the knives, and we scrubbed the big iron kettle above the furnace, washed and scalded the sausage grinder, and fastened it to the old sawhorse made especially for that purpose.

The children like to sit astraddle the sawhorse to turn the grinder. Yes, softhearted Nate lets them stay home from school to help and to watch, much to their delight. He claims it's just as educational as lessons at school, and I guess it is, too, in a way.

First thing in the morning, a fire is started in the big furnace in the washhouse, which is set up as a butcher shop for a few days. The water must be scalding hot. Rudy and Barbianne arrived to help, and Grandpa Dave and Grandma Annie wouldn't miss it for anything.

The carcasses are hung up, and later there are the hams and shoulders to trim and middlings to square. There's always much jovial bantering and visiting going on as we grind and slice and salt the meat and strip the fat for lard. The big hams and shoulders will be hung from the crossbeams in the smokehouse until they are cured and just the right flavor.

Visions of tender home-cured baked ham, juicy sausages, and crisp fried bacon dance in our heads as we work. Sadie saves the silky pigs' ears, and Peter and Crist the pigs' tails. They mischievously try to fasten them to the backside of Grandpa Dave without his knowing it, but he keeps a wary eye on them and shakes a bony finger at them if they try it.

The rendered lard is used to make doughnuts later. Barbianne and Dora work together at that, until the table is heaped high with the sweet, delectable, golden brown, yeasty-smelling temptations.

Little James likes them already! He was clinging to his mother's skirts and begging, until his daddy lifted him up high and gave him a taste. He doesn't want to be left out of the interesting goings-on.

At the end of the day, we divide the spoils. I think back to the last time Priscilla and Henry helped. How Martha would have loved butchering time.

Butchering also reminds me of something that happened in the 1800s, as told by an Amish man in a neighboring community. One morning before daybreak, his grandfather had gone to help a neighbor with the butchering. While the farmer finished the morning chores, the grandfather started the fire in the washhouse to heat the water for scalding the hogs.

Suddenly the farmer came running in, all excited and out of breath, crying, "The end of the world is coming. It is here! Just come to the door and see for yourself!"

The storyteller's grandfather rushed to the door and looked out. Imagine his astonishment when he saw that the stars were falling—falling like rain!

Some of the people knew they were not ready for the second coming of Christ, so they ran to the neighbors to make wrong things right. They wanted to ask to be forgiven, and to forgive one another. Some people could not stand the pressure, and there were a number of suicides.

The butchering was canceled, and the neighbors went home. But the end did not come.

It wonders me now if there would be a scientific explanation for a mass of falling stars like that. When Melvin heard the story, he checked in a library book and then told us he thought it was a meteor shower. Maybe God was using it to call people to repent and be ready to meet their Maker at any time. ✳

December 20

We're sure having our share of snow! During the night another winter snowstorm howled down from the north country and covered our valley with beautiful drifts of new-fallen snow.

School was canceled for the day, and we began our Christmas baking and candy making. Dora is also learning to sew. So from one end of the big kitchen came the whir of the treadle sewing machine, and from the other the good smells of Christmas cooking.

The heat from the old range kept us comfortable. The nearness of loved ones and the hum of the homey occupations brought a dear and pleasant feeling.

In the afternoon the wind stopped, and the sun came out. We bundled up and went for a tramp through the snow, following the creek and looking for the tracks of wild animals. Our snowshoes made tracks of their own.

We saw bunny tracks, lacy-looking bird tracks (or maybe it was mice), and even fox tracks. The drifted snow was pure white and breathtakingly beautiful, reminding me of the song, "Wash Me, and I Shall Be Whiter Than Snow."

Nate had supper ready when we came in, rosy-cheeked and famished. Tramping through the snow certainly whets one's appetite. Mush and eggs with sand tarts and hot chocolate sure tasted good even though it wasn't breakfast. I'm so glad he learned how to cook while he was still a bachelor. What a dear husband and father he is now!

This was another day of family togetherness, for my memory chest, one that I will cherish for a long time. Dora loved it, too. Tonight before bedtime, she came to me and said, a bit wistfully, "I wish life could always stay like this."

I felt a pang in my heart. She was standing before me in her nightgown, her big eyes in her heart-shaped face, looking so young and vulnerable.

A snatch of a song that Martha used to sing came to mind: "I'm just a child. My life is yet before me. I just don't know, what all that God has for me," or something like that. In a few years she will be old enough for *rum-schpringing* (running around with the youth). What does life have in store for her?

Will she choose to serve the Lord at an early age? Or will she sow wild oats for awhile first, as some do? We want to do all we can to teach her and guide her, so she will be able to resist worldly temptations. ❈

Interrogated

※ ※ ※ ※ ※ ※ ※ ※ ※ ※ ※

January 4

I have to think back to a year
ago when we had that mysterious prowler in our cellar.
Will we ever find out what that was all about, or will it always remain a mystery? Whoever it was didn't mean to
steal, for he left plenty of money.

Winter still has us in its icy grip. The children happily
go skating or sledding every evening after school. Then
they come in whining that they are cold and half starved.
At least that is something that is easily remedied. Are we
thankful enough that we have warm houses and plenty to
eat?

A row of pretty icicles hang from around the barn
eaves and from the porch roof. Peter brought one in tonight that was all of three feet long and clear as crystal. I
told him to gather more of them. We put them into a bur-
lap sack, smashed them up with the back of the ax, and
used them to make homemade vanilla ice cream.

It's too bad that there aren't icicles in summertime to
make ice cream with. In the winter we have to huddle
around the stove to get warm after eating it.

Rudy stopped in to chat a few minutes tonight and to
warm himself by the fire. Instead we chilled him by giving
him a bowl of ice cream.

He had news to tell us: Melvin took a girl home from

the singing on Sunday evening, but he hasn't found out yet who she is. Melvin is really secretive about it, so maybe Rudy will have to send out some scouters next time to see where he goes. I was hoping he would remain a bachelor so he could afford to keep on teaching. A good teacher isn't all that easy to find.

Tonight on our way in from the barn after chores, Sadie stopped to make a snow angel by lying on her back in the snow and sweeping her arms up over her head to make wings and spreading her legs to make the robe.

"That's for Amanda," she said matter-of-factly. And by the light of the low silvery moon on the horizon, it really did look like a shining angel. ▦

February 14

*V*alentine's Day. At school they had a Valentine's Day party of sorts. Each scholar took an ingredient for homemade raspberry ice cream—eggs, milk, sugar, cream, vanilla, instant clear gelatin, a jar of canned raspberries, and salt for freezing it. In the afternoon the girls mixed the ingredients in Eli's big twelve-quart, hand-cranked ice-cream freezer, while the boys went to the pond with an ax and a sack for the ice.

They all took turns cranking, and when it was done, they had an ice-cream party. Teacher Melvin treated them with heart-shaped cookies that Barbianne had made. After the treats were eaten, they passed out the homemade valentines.

Dora received a big red heart with white lace around the edge. On the back in a boy's handwriting was a poem:

Bunnies are cute,
So are squirrels.
But nothing beats
The Amish girls.

She came home with cheeks aflame and pretended to
be indignant. But when I was putting away the laundry tonight, I noticed that she had propped the valentine up in
front of the mirror on her dresser.

Peter tattled tonight at the supper table: "I know who
that valentine was from; it was Gideon. I know he likes
Dora. He gave her a piece of candy, too."

Dora had a fiery retort ready, and Nate made them
both be quiet.

Oh dear, another reminder that our little girl is growing up! We won't be able to keep her under our wings for
always. ✺

March 2

We're having temperatures
up to fifty degrees this week. A few days of heavy rains
caused all the winter snows to melt in a hurry. The result is
severe flooding in some areas.

Our creek is a roaring, raging river that is overflowing
its banks. It's rather awesome to stand close to the mighty
rushing waters and see the debris and huge logs bobbing
on the water, swept by as if they were weightless. The
white foam eddies and swirls around any obstacles in its
path.

This afternoon we got a notion to hitch up and drive to

the store for groceries. When we came to the bridge at Rudy's, the water was out over the banks and flowing completely over the road.

Nate decided that it couldn't be more than ten inches deep, and that we could safely ford it. But our horse was skittish. After gingerly stepping into the water, he stopped and began to back.

The carriage turned sideways, and the hind wheels got closer and closer to the ditch, till it was precariously close to the edge. Swirling muddy water was all around us!

I screamed, and Nate jumped out into the water and led the horse safely across. Next thing we would have been swept right into the creek!

On the way home I insisted that we go the long way around so we wouldn't have to go through that again. Later I heard that just a few miles from here, a horse and carriage tried to cross a bridge where the water was rushing over the road leading to the bridge. That rig was swept off the road and stranded in over four feet of water.

The couple in the carriage was rescued by boat, and the horse nearly drowned. The fire company was called and got them out somehow. That would've been a little too much adventure for me! ▦

April 16

Our no-church Sunday. I spent the forenoon writing letters to Henry and Priscilla and Martha. At least we can keep in touch by mail and remind them that they are in our thoughts and prayers.

Martha's "few months" are up, but she says nothing

about coming home anymore. She must like it in Africa.

This afternoon Sadie and I went for a walk along the creek, way back into the bushland. We found a bubbling spring we'd never seen before, and nearby bloomed bluebells and shy violets and forget-me-nots.

It was such a blessedly warm and wonderfully sweet-smelling day. In the trees the robins sang sweetly and joyously, and the red-winged blackbirds called from the reeds in the marshes.

Sunny yellow dandelions dotted the thick green grass. Nate's freshly plowed fields lay mellowing in the spring sunshine. Sadie gathered a bouquet of fragrant wildflowers to brighten our kitchen.

When we came within sight of our buildings on the way back, we saw a horse and carriage at our hitching rail. We hurried a bit faster, sorry to be missing company. When I opened the kitchen door, Marc Wellington came to the door, extended his hand, and said, with a chuckle, "Come right in. We're at home!"

What a surprise! Melvin had brought Marc over, and he and Nate were soon absorbed in a checker game. So Marc and I sat at the table visiting.

First thing, he started to talk about Martha Brunner. "Melvin said that Martha doesn't live with you anymore. He didn't get around to telling me where she is now."

When I told him that Martha was in Africa helping Priscilla and Henry, he stared at me open-mouthed for a long moment, then clapped his hands to his head.

"The fortune-teller!" he cried in amazement. "Remember what she said? She predicted that Martha would go to a foreign country and marry a dark-skinned native! Her prophecy is going to come true."

"Well, I sure hope not!" I replied. "Just because the first part of the prophecy came true doesn't mean that the second part will."

However, I can't help but think of her friend, Chad Budhram. How old is he anyway? Is he dark-skinned? Come to think of it, Martha never wrote anything about such things.

Melvin had to leave then, to go and see that girl of his tonight. She's Sarah, one of Ammon D.'s, a sweet and charming young lass. She's young enough that we can hope to have Melvin for our teacher for a few more years.

Marc agreed to stay for supper. He and Nate went outside to pitch quoits while I prepared it. After supper was over and the chores were done, we grownups sat on the porch rockers to visit.

It was such a fine, mild evening with spring peepers calling from the meadowlands. The air was fragrant with the moist, earthy scents of spring. The children were playing a lively game of ball tag on the lawn.

Marc said, "What I've really come for is to make a confession." He paused to let this sink in. "I was a boarder in your barn for several weeks, over a year ago."

We were astonished, to say the least!

"What was the big idea?" Nate asked in bewilderment. "You weren't hiding from the police, were you?"

Marc shook his head, "No, but I should have gone to the cops. I'll tell you how it was. My first day in this area, I was in the park in town, and I saw a youngster throwing bread to a beautiful Canadian goose. When the goose swam close, the boy chopped its head off with a long knife.

"I was so angry that I grabbed the knife from the boy

and began to beat him up. I gave him the beating of his lifetime. That was foolish of me, and now I know that I was breaking the law.

"The boy's buddy ran and told the boy's dad. Seeing the knife, he yelled for someone to call the police because there was a dangerous man with a knife in the park. A man came running with a gun, threatening to shoot me.

"I saw that I was in danger and that it would be their word against mine, so I fled. I was new in town and didn't want to get in trouble with the law. I hid behind bushes along an alleyway until after dark, then came out here and took refuge in your barn.

"I liked it there, and I wasn't too sure of myself doing missionary work. So I guess you could say I was imitating Jonah, playing hooky for awhile, running away from God's work. My missionary partner reported me missing in action. Since then, I've made peace with my church."

Marc added, "I want to make sure you were amply paid for all I 'stole' and ate while I was hiding out."

He pulled out his billfold and asked, "How much do I owe you for rent and for the food and milk?"

Nate, with a twinkle in his eye, replied. "Would manuring out the cow stable sound like a fair payment?"

That made Marc squirm a bit, but he agreed to it. He sounded relieved when Nate told him that he was just joking and that all was fair and square.

We enjoyed our visit with him. He is an intelligent and interesting conversationalist. I found myself thinking, a bit wistfully, what a fine couple Martha and Marc would have made. Will the fortune-teller's prediction really come true? How could she have guessed what might happen? ⌗

*T*he older one gets, the faster time seems to fly. We've been especially busy this summer, and the days fly by, one after the other, on work-laden wings and in swift succession.

Dora is a strong and capable helper. She industriously kneads the bread dough, hoes the garden, scrubs the floors, and helps with the canning. There's not a lazy bone in her body. Instead, we have to tell her to stop and rest every now and then, so she doesn't overdo herself.

Rudys are planning to go on a two-week trip to Michigan to visit her sister this fall. They asked to leave little James here with us then. That's something to look foreward to! He's such a lovable little chap. While they are gone, Melvin will do their chores and board with us.

Pamela was here today and gave us a stack of newspapers. We shred them and use them to bed our cattle. After she left, I scanned through them a bit. But reading about the crimes committed and the world's problems left me a bit depressed.

In the birth columns, I noticed that close to half of the mothers are single. In another article I read that over half of all marriages today end in divorce. The advice columnists claim to help solve people's problems. But they give counsel that we would consider a sin and shame. For example, they think it's okay for a couple to live together before marriage. It's the accepted thing and no longer considered a sin and a shame.

Will the same thing eventually happen to our people? Will these things creep in, then become more and more common, until finally they are not only tolerated but considered inevitable and not a sin and shame?

Are we thankful enough for our heritage and upbringing, where marriage vows are for life? The things pertaining to marriage are to be kept within its sacred ties only. Sin is still sin. Members who persist in sin are excommunicated and put into the ban until brought to repentance and amendment of life.

We must be a light to the world and do our part to be a good example. What will happen to our nation if the majority of the people no longer fear God? Will it crash and fall like the Roman Empire? God's divine blessing rests on the nation that adheres to his plan for families.

Where God's original institutions are not honored, there is blight and downfall. When strong family values and God-ordained moral laws are cast aside as narrow-minded and legalistic, there is bound to be a decline. ❄

August 30

I hurriedly finished the school sewing yesterday. This morning the children were off, starting a brand new term of learning, and not only from lessons and book learning. They also are getting experience in learning to cooperate and get along with others, to interact with others outside the family, and to learn to bow to another authority besides the parents.

We're thankful to still have Teacher Melvin, but we know sometime or other we'll have to look for another teacher now that Sarah has entered the picture. I doubt that we'll ever be able to find a replacement as good as Melvin.

We always have single teachers because we can't pay enough for a teacher to raise a family. Melvin and Sarah want to find a farm so they can raise their children properly and teach them responsibility.

Going by what I hear from other districts, we may have a hard time finding any teacher for our school. It's a big challenge, and not everyone has what it takes. Some prefer to go for higher-paying jobs, too. Oh well, we'll cross that bridge when we come to it.

The summer canning is just about wound up for now. Maybe I'll put away some grape juice and pears yet. Next on the list is making several pairs of *Latzhosse* (broadfall pants) for Nate.

That brings back memories of him the last time I made *Latzhosse* for him and was trying to think up manly compliments for Nate. Oh, how silly I was! I have to laugh at myself now. And then the *Glumbe* (lump) under his arm. I was scared skinny!

I thought I'd never take my husband for granted again, that I'd be the most devoted wife any man ever had. But alas, all too soon I found out how easy it is to fall short of my goal. How the grind of daily living and raising a family can take the shine off my lofty aspirations.

However, every morning is a fresh start. The mercy of the Lord is new every morning. If we have made a mistake or fallen into a rut, with each new sunrise we have the opportunity to try to do better, to grow in grace, and to abide in Christ.

Last night we all went for a boat ride after the work was finished. It was blessedly cooler by the water, and peaceful, too. An occasional leaf dropped into the murky water and floated by. We passed bushes loaded with *Hollerbiere* (elderberries). We'll have to tell Rudys because they want to pick some this year.

A muskrat jumped off the bank into the water and swam away from us, forming a *V* in the water. Twilight descended around us with all its peace and beauty. Then heat lightning began to flash far off in the west, lighting up the sky one moment, then leaving us in total darkness again.

The muted creak of the boat and the soft splash of the oars were the only sounds besides the buzzing night insects. When we got back, we sat on the porch, and Nate told stories from his childhood days until the children were too sleepy to keep their eyes open. Off to bed they went.

The contentment, beauty, and serenity of the evening was the perfect ending to the children's summer vacation from school. It was another evening for our memory chest.

October 27

*L*ittle James is here, and we have had to baby-proof our kitchen. He's a sweet little fellow. I'm reminded anew of the saying I once heard: "A house without a baby in it is like a face without a smile or a song without music."

The baby gets so much attention that I'm afraid he'll be completely spoiled by the time his parents come home in two weeks. He has at least a dozen words that he can say already, and he repeats everything we ask him to.

I have such a longing to see little Bathsheba and Miriam, too, once again. We miss a lot because we are so far

away from them. The pitter-patter of little footsteps, the childish prattle, the nighttime bottles, the diapers, and the baby talk—all brought back memories of Henry and Priscilla's girls, and renewed our *Heemweh* (homesickness). I hope we'll get to see them again before they grow up.

The windmill is clanging tonight. A harvest wind has sprung up, and the copper moon hangs low on the horizon. A neighbor's dog is howling mournfully. A lonely feeling visits me when I'm thinking of loved ones far away.

I've given up expecting that Martha will ever come back to live with us. I wonder if her friend Chad that she writes so much about has anything to do with it. ▦

*T*he children have all been so eager to do things for little James. They lavish so much love and attention on him that it amuses me sometimes, but warms my heart. They really go out of their way to entertain him and care for him.

This morning after breakfast, an unfortunate thing happened. When Crist tried to lift James from his high chair, somehow he accidentally dropped him. *Ach mei!* Little James hit the tray, and then the floor, with his little arm pinned underneath him.

I carefully lifted the screaming little boy and saw that his arm hung crooked. Oh dear! I could have cried with him, but I didn't want to scare the children. What will Rudy and Barbianne think that we didn't take better care of their son?

Crist had a stricken look on his face, and I pitied him, too, that he was the one to drop the baby. We could see right away that the arm needed a doctor's attention. Dora ran over to Pam's to see if she could take us to the clinic.

Meanwhile I rocked James and sang to him, but he just cried and cried. Poor little boy! Pam came, and carried him to the car, and we were soon being ushered into the doctor's office.

There was a new, young doctor on duty, one that I'd never seen before. But it was a relief to hand James over to him and the nurses, knowing they could give him something to relieve the pain. They X-rayed the arm.

Twice the doctor asked me to explain how it had happened. Twice I told him everything. Yet he kept looking at me strangely with a skeptical look on his face.

127

He quizzed me again: "You say your son dropped him? How far did he fall?"

When I told him, he shook his head and muttered something to the nurse so softly that I didn't catch it. I was quite puzzled. Why were they acting so secretive and standoffish?

The doctor said, "This is a very bad break and could not have happened by falling just a few feet. And it's at a place where arm injuries usually happen when a child is physically abused."

His words and the meaning behind them didn't sink in right away. But when they did, I was shocked and horrified beyond words. They thought that we had deliberately injured little James!

Tears of anger, frustration, and hurt stung my eyes at the unfairness of his assumption and the coldness and hardness of his tone of voice. I was just dumbfounded at the injustice of his suspicions.

When he said they were going to put James to sleep to set the arm and to check for other injuries, I wanted to sob like little James had. I think I was more hurt and angry than I'd ever been before.

A nurse told me to follow her into another room. She told me to wait there until somebody came. There I sat and sat, wondering if they had called the police, whether they would soon handcuff me and take me to prison.

What a hopeless and helpless feeling it was! I was stung to the quick and desperately wished Pam could be in the room with me. She could have told that *grosshunsich* (uppity) doctor a thing or two!

After what seemed like a long time, the door opened, and the nurse ushered in a man and a woman. They were from Children's Social Services, and the cross-examining began. They kept questioning me until I was utterly disgusted and weary. How could such a terrible thing have happened?

They finally stopped the interrogation and left. After another long wait, they came back and said they decided to let me take the baby home. However, someone not of our household would have to be there the whole time and overnight.

Then they said that tomorrow they'd come to our house to look things over and make sure the baby was safe. Oh, the utter humiliation of it all!

I was trembling with something between indignation and fear. When they brought the sleeping James to me with a cast on his arm, I was almost too weak to carry him.

Then and ever since, it has seemed like a nightmare, and it's not over yet. Pam nearly had a fit when she heard about it, in the car on the way home. In spite of myself, I had to laugh at her reaction.

Nate took it quite calmly, saying that he's sure our name will be cleared. I certainly felt a lot better after pouring out my tale of woe to him.

To fulfill the condition laid down, Grandpa Daves spent the rest of the day here and are here for the night. It sure made them talk, too. Dave can really spout off when he's upset about something. And what, oh what, would Rudy and Barbianne think if they knew? I'm sure they wouldn't be able to enjoy the rest of their trip at all.

I don't expect to be able to get much sleep tonight. James will be waking up often. I dread of having those people snooping around our house tomorrow. And I am wondering what the verdict will be.

I find myself praying, "Please, God, let those people understand that it could have happened the way I told them, for it was the truth. Let our name be cleared of the false blame and charges." But I know I will find rest and peace when I stop my frantic praying and instead joyously thank God that he will take care of everything according to his will. "Casting all your care upon him; for he cares for you." ▦

November 3

*O*ur ordeal is over at last! What a relief. No Social Services people showed up at our home. But in the afternoon we had another appointment at the clinic for James. There they were, ready to fire more questions at us, and they kept at it until we were called into the doctor's office.

What a relief to find our usual doctor in today. He was kind and understanding and did all he could to get those Social Services people to drop the case. But they weren't satisfied to drop it until they would see where it happened.

They followed us home, looked at the high chair, and questioned Crist, who had just come home from school. Then finally they reluctantly agreed that it could have happened the way we said it did.

After they left, we sat visiting with Grandpa Dave and Grandma Annie, feeling drained and relieved. We felt a lot more mellow toward those government people than we did yesterday. I suppose at the hospital and the clinic they get too many cases of actual child abuse, and that's why they have to be so suspicious. They were only doing their job.

I guess we have to admit that we were hurt that we weren't trusted and taken for Christian people. But perhaps they've learned not to trust anybody, for anyone can lose control.

"All is well that ends well" (Heywood), and we are truly thankful to God for delivering us. ⌗

A day of golden, mellow sunshine. I spent some time raking leaves, with little James toddling around and playing in the piles. His cast doesn't seem to hinder him much anymore, and he doesn't seem to have any pain. My, those little bones must heal fast!

We're all enjoying him so much again since he's feeling better. Dora has taken over the care of him in the evening, fixing his bottle and getting him into his pajamas.

I'm sure that she misses Miriam Joy and little Bathsheba more than she cares to admit. It doesn't seem fair that they have to be separated. Hopefully, someday soon they'll come home, and then she can again spend as much time with them as she wants.

Peter and Crist play peekaboo and hide-and-seek games with James. They go through all kinds of funny antics to make him laugh. He does have such a merry, rollicking, infectious giggle!

Sadie loves to show him picture books. It sounds so cute when he tries to repeat all the words she says and even make the animal sounds. But in a few days Rudy and

Barbianne will be back, and then our little baby sunbeam will go home.

I wonder, How will the parents' faces look when they see that little cast on his arm? Maybe we should have let them know, but it sure would've spoiled their trip. ▦

November 9

*W*e had an all-day, pouring rain. It splashed against the windowpanes, on the roof, and into the gutters, filling our cistern. Before suppertime, the rain stopped, and the sun came out for a short time, lighting up the old world with a beautiful rainbow, fully visible from one end to the other. Right under the arch came Rudy's black horse prancing in the lane, pulling their carriage.

In a few moments Barbianne fairly flew up the walk and into the kitchen. Dora had lifted James to the window to see them coming. When Barbianne reached out to take James from her, he seemed undecided for an instant. It almost seemed like he would shrink back and cling to Dora, but then his face broke into a smile, and he reached for Barbianne with both arms.

Only then did she notice the cast. By this time Rudy had tied the horse and was coming in, too. We had quite a story to tell. Was there ever a baby that was loved and hugged more?

We persuaded them to stay for supper, for Melvin had done their chores. They accepted gladly. I prepared a double recipe of yummasetti (noodles and hamburger), and Dora had apple dumplings baking in the oven.

Grandpa Daves must have seen Rudy's carriage passing. Right after supper, they came over, too, and we had an old-time visit. Whenever we get together like that, there's always an ache that won't go away. Before they left, Priscilla, Henry, and the girls were part of our jolly group. We're missing Martha a lot, too. She and "Grampie" sure loved to tease each other. I try to remind myself that they are doing a good work there in Africa, and if even just one soul should be saved, it would be worthwhile. ▦

December 22

*J*oyous Christmas season! This year Teacher Melvin had a real Christmas program at school—one of the best I ever attended. Gideon (the giver of Dora's valentine) is a natural-born narrator, and he was the life of the party.

The scholars had exchanged names, and we watched as each child happily unwrapped a gift. Teacher Melvin had Dora's name. He gave her a book entitled *The Home Beautiful*. It looks interesting and helpful, and I'm anxious to find time to read it.

Each family had brought along cookies, which we set out and served with hot chocolate, while visiting after the program. Teacher Melvin gave each of the children a small bag of candy and an orange.

When we left the schoolhouse, snowflakes were falling, and the children greeted them with shouts of joy. It has been snowing ever since, so we'll probably have a white Christmas.

Melvin is hitching two workhorses to the big bobsled.

The *Yunge* (youths) of *rumschpringing* age (sixteen years old and up) want to go Christmas caroling tonight. Melvin filled the box of the sled with plenty of straw for them to sit on. How Martha would have loved that!

I wonder what she and Henrys are doing tonight. Maybe I have a bit of *Heemweh* for them. Do Africans celebrate Christmas, too? We shipped them a big box of homemade gifts and cookies, and sent along best wishes for a blessed Christmas. I hope it arrives in time. ✶

YEAR SIXTEEN

Changes

*W*hen the days do lengthen, the cold does strengthen. We had a genuine old-fashioned blizzard on Sunday, with drifts as high as the fenceposts in some places. The wind, with its icy breath, howled around the house and mounted up drifts with a white fury, then shrieked around the barn, too. I wonder what the poor little winter birds do for shelter.

On Monday morning the sun shone brightly on all that pristine loveliness, giving it a dazzling brightness. The creek is like a winding silver ribbon.

I finally found time on Sunday to read part of Dora's book, *The Home Beautiful.* There is much good reading in it, and perhaps I'll copy parts of it in my journal.

Some of chapter 7 is written for those who have lost a child and experienced the sorrow of parting with a loved one. It speaks of years of unbroken gladness. The stream of family life has flowed so long with merry ripples through the green fields, amid the flowers, and the bright sunshine. Then it sweeps into the deep shadows, plunges into the dark and sunless gorge, or is hurled over the waterfall.

We press our children to our bosoms today. Love builds up a thousand brilliant hopes for them in our hearts. Yet tomorrow death comes, and they lie silent and

137

still amid the flowers. The author tells of things that comfort us. One of them is the truth of immortal life. In the autumn, birds leave our chilly northern zone, and we hear their songs no more.

However, the birds are not dead. In the warm southern climate, amid flowers and fragrant foliage and luscious fruits, they are still singing as happily as they warbled for us in summer. So our children leave us. We miss their sweet faces and prattling voices, but they have gone to the summer-land of heaven. There they dwell in the midst of the glory of the Lord, anointing other hearts with their tender grace.

There is much comfort in this counsel if we can know with the heart that it is so. I like to think of Amanda in the summer-land of heaven, and I want to share this with Barbianne, too. ▦

February 17

*W*e received a letter from Martha today. As usual, her letter was much more newsy and informative than Priscilla's are. It seems as if both Henry and Priscilla hold us at arm's length. Do they delight in being uninformative and secretive? Or do I just feel that way? Maybe they are just too busy.

Martha began her letter with the usual "*Jambo*" which must be a greeting in the Swahili language. Her letters are full of Chad Budhram. She and Chad visited Victoria Falls together. The way Martha wrote, this is something that would outshine and outroar Niagara Falls.

They stopped in front of a mud brick house with a

thatched roof. The family invited them to stay and eat a meal with them. They consented; and were served *ugali* (something made out of corn flour) and *lenga lenga* (a boiled stew with red-stemmed pigweed in it. The family called them *muzungu*, which means "foreign stranger."

She wrote that she has taught Chad to speak both German and Pennsylvania Deitsch. He already knew English, and he has taught her his native tongue. I'm impressed. That must've been quite an accomplishment!

At the end of her letter, she wrote, "I love Africa, but I'm getting lonesome for you all. Sometime soon I'm coming back to you, and I'm bringing Chad along."

Her promise didn't impress me much; she has said that much before. So I doubt that she'll ever come back, especially with Chad. Oh well, she was a golden sunbeam in our home while she was here, and we'll cherish her stay for always. 🕸

March 23

*H*ousecleaning time. Pam stopped in while I was scrubbing floors and handed me a fat package.

"My finished manuscript," she explained. "Do you want to read it now or later?"

"Now, of course!" I responded. I knew she had been working on that novel for seven years!

I couldn't resist looking at it, at least. When I had started it, I simply couldn't put it down. So there went my day of housecleaning.

It was such an absorbing true-to-life story, set in the

Civil War period. How does she write so well? I guess it's her college education and her natural-born talent with words. But I just don't understand how anyone could know enough about life back then, or be able to plot the story and develop the characters like she does. Pam sure has a knack for choosing words and putting them together.

I've often wondered whether Pam ever again put an ad in the paper for companionship, or whether her date with George squelched that idea. She hasn't said a word about it since. Maybe she was too absorbed in finishing her book.

She stopped in tonight again. I returned her manuscript and told her I wouldn't be a bit surprised if we'd lose our good neighbor once her book is on the best-seller list and she is among the elite and famous.

"There's no chance of that," Pam replied. "I'm not even sure it will be accepted. I'll be sitting on pins and needles until I hear from the publishers. It wouldn't be the first time I'd see a rejection slip."

Well, I'm sure she needn't worry. If I know anything, that book will be a hit. ❖

April 10

*D*ora's birthday, and now she's a teenager. She got a card in the mail, a birthday greeting with no name, with only a verse printed on it: "Roses are red, Violets are blue, Sugar is sweet, And so are you."

The handwriting was the same as on her valentine

card a year ago. Well! It's high time we put a stop to this! I had just taken the valentine as a school joke, but now I am concerned. I hope she hasn't been doing anything out of the way to encourage him.

Tonight as we got ready for bed, I told Nate about it. He took a milder view of it. "Let them go, and they'll forget about it before long. If we try to interfere, it will just make them more determined. Besides, aren't you glad she's not in Africa with an African for a friend, like Martha does?"

Well yes, of course. But she's not even *rumschpringing* (going out with the youth) yet. Maybe Nate is right. By the time the youngsters are sixteen, they'll have forgotten all about it. I was hoping she would stay a little girl awhile yet. ▦

May 12

*B*eautiful blossom time! The lilac bush is laden with fragrant lavender bouquets. The fruit trees are in various stages, each with their own special beauty and fragrance.

A cardinal is singing from the pine tree these days. His "pretty, pretty, pretty," then "good cheer, good cheer, good cheer" is a welcome part of the bird chorus in the morning. I hope they build a nest there.

The garden is as pretty as a picture. Leaf lettuce and radishes are ready. Maybe next week the carrots will be big enough to start using them as we thin out the rows. The peas look nice, and also the potatoes. I hope I can keep the garden as weedfree all summer as it is now.

Dora and Sadie planted all the flowers yesterday after school. Then this morning they neatly mulched the flower beds. Peter and Crist pushed the clattering mower over the yard and cut the grass.

When Nate came in from the barn for dinner, he complimented us: "It looks like you have the place all spruced up and ready for company."

The words were barely out of his mouth when there came a knock at the front door. Before we could answer, the door opened and Martha walked in, smiling and vivacious as ever, followed by a tall, dark-skinned African young man.

"This is my friend, Chad Budhram," she said, a bit proudly, or maybe possessively. "Or rather, I should say, he's more than a friend. We're engaged to be married, maybe next year."

Nate shook hands with Chad, but I'm afraid I merely stood there staring at him for a few moments. I had suspected as much, but to see him here—with Martha so fair, and him so dark-skinned—was a shock.

"Well, say something!" Martha blurted out, almost impatiently. "Can't you at least congratulate us?"

I found my voice then and gave them a proper welcome, I hope. Then I bustled around, putting two more plates at the table, and going to the cellar and pantry for more food.

At the dinner table, Martha explained how they sneaked in like that without us seeing them coming. They had walked across the field from Rudy's place. Actually, they walked from the bus stop in town and stopped off at Rudy's first.

Chad is a real gentleman. I believe he's as good-natured as Martha claimed in her letters. He is courteous and soft-spoken, and he speaks Pennsylvania Deitsch amazingly well. It's unbelievable that he could have learned so much in just the two years that Martha was in Africa. I don't believe Henry and Priscilla bothered to teach him Deitsch. He must be a fast learner.

As soon as Chad and Martha had told us about their trip home, we began to ply them with questions about Henry, Priscilla, and the girls. We were happy to hear that they are fine and doing well there in Africa. Best of all, they are coming home to stay in a few years. I am so glad, especially for Dora's sake. When Dora heard it, she left the table —I'm sure so that the others wouldn't see her tears of joy.

After dinner Dora and Sadie left to baby-sit James while Barbianne went to town to do some shopping. The menfolk sat on the porch to visit.

Martha and I were left alone to clear the table and do the dishes. The first thing she asked was, "Have you heard of Marc since I left?"

So I told her of Marc's visit, and that he mentioned that it looks like the fortune-teller's prediction would be fulfilled.

Martha nodded soberly. "Maybe there *is* an occult power in it. I won't go to a place like that ever again.

"As for marrying an African, such a thing was farthest from my mind when I left here. I never thought I'd fall in love with an African, but I did. Chad is a Christian, and I know we were meant for each other."

I couldn't resist asking, "Was it love at first sight, too, like you said about Marc?"

Martha shrugged her shoulders and tossed her pony-tail. "Oh that! That wasn't real love, just infatuation. I didn't fall in love with Chad right away. But I was working with him day after day there at the clinic where we both were nurse's aides. I saw how kindhearted and gentle he was with the patients. That just won my heart over."

Well, I am concerned, to say the least. Do they realize what problems a mixed-race marriage would bring? I'd like to remind her that she once declared that she won't get married before she was twenty-five. Why doesn't she stick to that?

Maybe later she'll decide that what she feels for Chad was just an infatuation, too. But I know it wouldn't do a bit of good for me to suggest that.

Martha asked to board with us again. She wants to wear her Amish clothes to show Chad. They asked Rudy and Barbianne if Chad could board with them, but their answer was that one boarder is enough. Melvin is already there. So Chad has gone to town to look for a room to rent.

I wonder, What was the real reason Rudys declined? I'm afraid it will take awhile for us to get used to Chad's dark color. 🎴

May 16

*I*t's so good to have our bouncy, bubbly sunbeam back. She goes to the barn to greet all the animals, talking to them and petting them, treating them like old friends. On Monday she returns to her old job, but this week she's here getting reacquainted with us.

It was really amusing to see Chad's face yesterday afternoon when he came over and saw Martha wearing her

Amish clothes and *Kapp*. He had the most startled look on his face! Martha coquettishly paraded around in front of him, laughingly showing off.

Oh dear, I still think it can't be! I don't believe they understand what a serious step they will be taking if they do get married. Their children would never really fit in anywhere, would they? Yet as impulsive as Martha is, maybe they'll have a spat and "fall out" yet before they get that far. But then again, as easygoing as Chad is, that's not likely to happen either.

Today I asked Martha how long she and Chad will be staying before they go back to Africa.

"We're not going back," she replied, "at least not to live. We're making our home right here in this community."

Then, with a mischievous twinkle in her eyes, she said, "Don't be surprised if we even decide to join the Amish. Chad thinks it's great seeing a horse and buggy traveling along a country road. He could make himself right at home with you people."

Nate had just come in and heard the latter part of the conversation. So she asked him, "Do you think the preachers would allow a person of a different race to join?"

Without thinking, he replied, "Of course not."

Then, seeing the astonished look on Martha's face, he quickly added, "I guess you'll have to ask them if it wonders you."

I told her, "Don't worry. Such a thing has never happened, and it probably never will, but I don't believe anyone would be turned away because of the color of their skin, if they would believe in Christ and conform to the *Ordnung* (church rules)."

145

"But maybe not if they planned a mixed marriage," Nate added. "I doubt that they would approve of that."

Martha set her lips in a tight line and said no more, but her eyes said plenty.

Later she told me, "I think Nate is just prejudiced. Surely the ministers wouldn't feel that way. I just can't understand how someone could be that . . . uh . . . unyielding.

"After all, Philip baptized the Ethiopian eunuch. And an African helped Jesus bear the cross on the way to Calvary. Do you think Jesus would have turned anyone away because of their color?"

"No, of course not," I told her. "But you aren't planning to join, so why worry?"

"Who knows?" Martha protested. "And I just have to know. You can't imagine how that would hurt me to know that you people would simply not accept a sincere believer of a different color."

"It wouldn't be just the ministers' decision," I explained. "Their proposal would have to be tested by the *Gmeerot* (counsel of the church). It's not that Chad would be rejected for his race or color. But they might feel that a mixed marriage is not God's will, or not fair to the children. Would the children ever really be completely accepted in our country?"

Martha sobered. "I've thought of that," she said quietly. "What's more important—would they be accepted in our church? But we could always go back to Africa to live if they were treated unfairly here."

There, she said it! I sure hope she counts all the costs carefully before she takes the step. It seems to me like a very weighty decision to make. But it's her life, and she'll have to live with the decision. ❋

We had church services at Rudy's place, and Chad and Martha attended. It caused quite a stir when Chad walked in with the men. I wonder what he thought of the slow tunes sung, the backless benches, the simple meal of bread, the church spread, with red beets and pickles, smearcase, tea, and *Schnitzboi* (pie made from dried apples).

Nate said that Chad is an interesting talker. He was the center of attention in the afternoon when the men were sitting in a circle out under the shade tree and visiting. We stayed for supper, as did Chad and Martha and a few other neighbors.

In the evening, both the men and the women sat out under the shade tree to visit. Martha took that as an opportunity to ask Preacher Emanuel for his opinion on interracial marriages.

Emanuel removed the toothpick from his mouth, leaned back in his chair, and replied, "Whether that is right or wrong is not for me to say. But, tell me, did you ever see a bluebird and a purple martin building a nest together and raising young?"

Martha didn't reply, but she seemed deep in thought. I'm so glad that Emanuel didn't condemn them outright. Maybe it would be a good idea for Martha to talk with other couples of different races who have taken the step of marriage. Would they recommend it for others, or do it over again?

I think Martha has fully made up her mind. Maybe she is feeling a bit defensive or wants to be affirmed in her decision.

Tonight, in the pleasant, fragrant evening air, I walked out to the garden with Sadie, and we found a few ripe strawberries! The sugar peas are bulging, too, so that means good eating and busy days ahead. Later we sat on the porch glider in the dusky twilight, with a warm summer breeze shaking the leaves and making the moonbeams twinkle.

Nate and the boys joined us, too. Martha and Chad had gone for a walk. Dora was spending the night with her friend, Eli's Rachel, which I suppose is a taste of things to come, when she starts *rumschpringing*.

I felt a twinge of sadness. All too soon she'll be away on Sunday evenings, then next will be Peter, then Sadie, then Crist. One by one they'll grow up and leave home. Then Nate and I will be alone—but they'll come back to visit, with our grandchildren!

Such is life, full of changes, sunshine and shadows, joys and sorrows. What will life hold for each of them? It's a comforting thought to know that God is their heavenly Father and Christ is their guide.

If they do not stray away from Christ, he will be there to lift them up when they stumble and fall, to lead them in the paths of righteousness, and on to that eternal home where sin and sorrow cannot enter, and all tears shall be wiped away.

Our little Amanda is already safe in that heavenly home. Now that the pain of parting with her has subsided, we can truly say, "The Lord gave, and the Lord has taken away; blessed be the name of the Lord," and mean it from the heart. ❖

Our no-church Sunday. We took our lunch down to the creek and spread it on a tablecloth with our carriage blankets nearby for us to sit on or lie down, as we pleased. Dora brought a bouquet of pink roses for a centerpiece and pinned a rose on her cape.

The roses this year are the most beautiful and fragrant ever, or do I say that every year? I have to think of the epitaph: "If you ever doubt there is a God, look deep into a rose." How could anyone fail to be reminded of the Creator?

After lunch was over, Nate took a nap and the girls went for a walk. The boys played in the water, piling up stones for another swimming hole.

I had Dora's book along that Teacher Melvin gave her for Christmas. It has much fine thought and advice in it. I came to a portion that Dora had underlined. It must have impressed her. I will share some of its wisdom here.

The section tells of flowers giving out perfume only when crushed, and odoriferous wood releasing fragrance when an ax hews it. Likewise, Jesus yielded tender love to the rough impact of others' rudeness.

We should strive to fashion our character by that model. An ugly disposition mars the loveliness of the pattern we want to shape in our souls.

Some people keep hurting others, even their truest friends. Some are sulky and cast a chilling shadow over a whole household. Others are so sensitive, watching for slights and offended by trifles. Others are so quarrelsome that the meekest person cannot live peaceably with them.

How can a bad-tempered person become good-tempered? There is no character so bad that it cannot be turned into sweetness. The grace of God can transform the worst life into the image of Christ. It goes on to say how this is done.

I wonder why this portion impressed Dora. Does she feel the need of being transformed into the image of Christ? I've noticed a refinement in her personality of late, a gentleness and winsomeness that wasn't there before, and my heart rejoices and is made glad.

Peter, Sadie, and Crist are just a few years behind Dora. If she would be a bad example to them, willful and head-strong or determined to sow wild oats, might they not want to follow in her footsteps? I'm so thankful that she is being a good example.

Chad and Martha joined us later in the afternoon by the creek. They sat on a fallen log to visit with us until it was time to start the chores. Chad stayed for supper, and he and Martha went for a boat ride tonight.

We sat on the porch and watched the twilight stealing over the lovely, misty meadowlands. The fireflies were out, and the bullfrogs croaking their throaty, poignant song. The cows were making their way back to the meadow for their evening grazing, and the birds were tittering a sleepy good-night.

Ah, sweet summertime sounds and scenes! ▦

June 28

Gloria Graham paid me another visit tonight. It's been a while since she was here. I guess she gave up trying to make me over. She hasn't said anything lately about me wearing light-colored dresses or using her diet product.

However, she had big news for us tonight. They're moving to Arizona! George has asthma and prefers a drier climate. They're pulling up stakes completely and selling the house which Henry and Priscilla had lived in. She asked us to come and visit them after they're settled in their new home.

As a whole, they've been good neighbors to us. Before Pam was here, they did a lot for us, too. I wonder if they would appreciate it if we'd have a farewell singing or gathering for them. And also, I guess we should notify Henry and Priscilla. If they have plans to come back soon, they might want to buy the house. I sure hope so.

July 4

*T*he *Englischer* (non-Amish) are having a holiday today, and there was a big celebration in town last night. We climbed the barn hill and watched the fireworks exploding and the spectacular displays of color and design in the sky. It seemed as if no two were alike.

This morning Pam stopped in for milk, and she said that over five thousand dollars was spent on those fireworks. Whew! They could have looked at the stars and spent that money on something else!

We've really been thankful for Chad's help with our farmwork this summer. Melvin went home to work for his dad this summer. Then Rudy couldn't work for a few weeks because of an infection in his foot from stepping on a rusty nail, which pierced his rubber boot and his foot.

Chad helped with the haymaking, and Nate said he stacks those heavy bales like they're almost weightless. So he is strong and apparently used to hard work. He'd probably make a good farmer. He's going to help with the threshing too, then find himself a job in town. The boys are growing up and able to do a lot, but at the busiest times, we still need an extra hand.

Dora is helping Barbianne a lot this summer. That is good for Sadie, because then she takes more responsibility on herself and takes hold of the work better.

Martha works around here all she can in the evenings when she comes home from her job. That gave us a lift during the busy strawberry and pea season.

Last night as we were snapping green beans for canning, we started talking about her engagement to Chad. It seems like they are both having second thoughts and have agreed together to put the engagement on hold for awhile, maybe even for a few years.

I'm sure glad to hear that, for they're both young yet, maybe too young to fully count the costs. If they would marry in haste, they might repent at leisure, as the proverb goes. ⌘

July 5

After a good refreshing rain last night, the corn in the fields is growing by leaps and bounds. The old saying calls for it to be "knee high by the fourth of July," but it's closer to waist high this year.

Today we had our first meal of sweet corn from the

garden. Mmmmm, was it ever delicious! Now I can hardly wait for those delicious ripe tomatoes and new lima beans and potatoes. Fresh raspberries, crisp head lettuce, and cabbage are also on the menu.

City folks who can't have a garden sure miss out on a lot. What one buys at the grocery stores can't begin to compare with the fresh produce straight out of the garden.

I had a letter from Polly today. Her letters never fail to cheer and inspire, and sometimes to amuse. She had enclosed her "Garden Plan," and I thought it was good:

First plant five rows of peas:
   Piety   Prudence   Prayer   Purity   Praise
Next plant five rows of squash:
   Squash Idleness   Squash Gossip   Squash Unkindness
   Squash Self-indulgence   Squash Pride
Then plant five rows of lettuce:
   Let-us-be-humble   Let-us be-faithful
   Let-us-be-unselfish   Let-us-be-loving
   Let-us-be-sanctified
And to make all things count for something good and worthwhile, no garden is complete without turnips:
   Turn-up-for-church-services
   Turn-up-to-go-the-second-mile
   Turn-up-with-a-cheerful-smile
   Turn-up-with-a-willing-mind

She wrote that she had seen a similar piece in a circle letter, but she changed the wording to suit herself. That garden produce certainly describes Polly herself.

Polly also wrote that they just had their tenth grandchild. Rachel's first baby, born a few days ago, is a little girl named Polly! I'd sure like to go and see that little miss, even though it is a twelve-mile drive.

Next she hinted that "little" Mary might be getting married before long. Can it really be possible? Time sure doesn't stand still.

I'll always cherish the memories of working for that family. Their gentle old grandmother and her serene influence was such a blessing to us all. I hope if I ever get to be old, I can be just like her. ▦

*O*ur boys have been taking turns helping Rudy this spring and summer, every morning and evening. To show appreciation, he gave them a pick from the litter of his purebred Irish Setter puppies.

They chose Rusty, a beautiful pup with the most trusting, loyal expression on his face. He is as devoted to the boys as they are to him. We've been without a dog on the farm now for awhile, and I believe it is true, that every boy needs a dog to love and care for.

When we go for walks in the meadow, Rusty already scents out the rabbit trails and chases them into the thickets. Then he comes back matted with cockleburs. Sometimes a bunny springs out right under his nose, and off he goes after him.

The boys can hardly wait until fall when the pheasant season opens. They think he'll be an excellent bird dog, too. I guess he will if he flushes out the pheasants as well as he does the rabbits.

In the evening, when the day's work is done, the boys

romp and play with him on the lawn. I rejoice to hear them and thank God that they are fine, sturdy, and healthy. I pray that they will be strong enough to say no to worldly temptations and that they'll lead fine, exemplary lives that are a good example to others. ⌗

September 21

*F*irst day of autumn. My, the summer again flew by as if on wings. A busy, happy summer it was, with Dora and Martha here only in the evening, and Chad coming to visit every weekend.

It does one good to have young people around with their optimistic outlook on life, their cheerful bantering back and forth, and their camaraderie. According to Martha, she and Chad are "just friends" now. What the outcome of that will be, I don't know.

The nights are turning cool, so we start a fire in the range in the morning and evening. The canning is done, and once again we have a friendly cricket chirping in the kitchen.

Soon the corn will be cut and we can say that the "frost is on the punkin and the fodder's in the shock" (Riley).

The leaves will be turning brilliant with rich scarlet and warm gold and dull brown. After the work is done, fall is a good time of year. The cellars and barns and silos are filled, the harvest is over, and we count our blessings and remember to thank God for his goodness.

On Saturday evening we had our neighborhood farewell gathering here for Gloria and George before they start for Arizona. Rudys were here, and Pam, and Grandpa Daves and Eli's family, and Martha and Chad.

Barbianne wanted to make part of the meal, so I let her make a haystack supper, something that is becoming quite popular among our people. I'll copy the recipe here so I won't forget it.

Hay Stack

Ritz crackers	taco sauce
cooked rice	tomatoes
corn chips or tortilla chips	
lettuce and shredded carrots	
hamburger, plus onions to taste	cheese sauce

Crush the crackers, cook the rice, and crush the corn chips. Brown the hamburger and onions. Add taco sauce and chunked tomatoes. Cut up the lettuce. Put on top of each other in the order given. When done, pour cheese sauce over top of the big stack. Delicious!

We all truly thought it was delicious and proved that by eating heartily. For dessert, we made a freezer full of vanilla ice cream (with ice bought in town) and served it with shoofly pie.

Gloria asked us to sing a few slow tunes after supper, from the *Ausbund* (the hymnal we use in church). We gladly did so. Then Gloria and George even sang a song for us. It sounded just like a radio song we sometimes hear over the radio in stores.

Martha then asked "Grampie" to tell some of his stories. Grandpa Dave kept us entertained for the rest of the evening.

Before they left for home, Gloria and George urged us all to come and visit them once they are in Arizona. I suppose we'll think of them this winter when the icy winds howl down from the mountains and the snow covers our valley. They'll be out basking in seventy- or eighty-degree sunshine. At least that's what they claim the winters are like there, pleasant and mild.

As for me, I don't think I'd like to live where there's no real winter. Spring wouldn't seem nearly as enchanting and lovely as it does after a real winter.

Before they leave, their house will be secured for Henrys to use when they come back. Oh, I can hardly wait to see them again! ✣

November 16

We've been having cold, gray, dreary November days. The trees seem stark and lifeless, and the water flowing between the creek banks is chilly, dark, and brooding.

Oh well, we had a lovely autumn with many a sunshiny, mellow Indian summer day to finish the fall work and the housecleaning.

Last week we had a letter from Isaac and Rosemary Bontrager with the exciting news that their son Matthew will be coming for a visit! He will be attending a cousin's wedding in the area. I haven't seen him since we were out to Minnesota to visit them, quite a few years ago.

At first Isaac and Rosemary had planned to come, too, bringing all eight of their children along, but plans changed at the last minute. That sure made me sorry. I wanted to hear Isaac preach once again.

We weren't sure which day Matthew would come, either before or after the wedding; then yesterday morning he unexpectedly came to the door in time for breakfast. My, I wouldn't have known him anymore! He's six feet tall and well-built, and his hair has turned darker. His expression and smile bear a resemblance to the little Matthew, though. That brought back a flood of memories from when he was a motherless toddler and called me "Mammie."

The way these children grow up so fast sure has a way of making us feel old. Matthew helped buzz wood all forenoon and stayed for dinner. In the afternoon, Nate and the boys took him to visit some Beiler cousins on his mother's side of the family.

I've been thinking a lot about the days when I worked for Isaac after Elizabeth, his first wife, died when Matthew was an infant. I feel glad that things turned out so well for him, that he got a good wife like Rosemary.

Priscilla, who had kept company with Isaac for a while

after his first wife died, turned out a lot better than I thought she would. But there just aren't many that can compare to Rosemary. She was the perfect *Schtiefmammi* (stepmother) for Matthew, too, a real mother, and a good minister's wife. ▦

December 22

I wonder, amid all this going to Christmas dinners, cooking, baking, candy making, and gift wrapping and exchanging: Do we stop often enough to ponder the real meaning of Christmas? Do we prepare our hearts to make room for Christ? Or do we turn him away, like Mary and Joseph were turned away at the inn? Do we celebrate X-mas with Christ left out, or Christmas with Christ at the center of our lives and hearts?

We're having Christmas dinner at our house this year, and Martha is wholeheartedly involved in preparing for it. She even skipped going to the school program yesterday. When I came home, the table was piled high with crisp, golden-brown doughnuts. She enlisted the girls' aid for dipping them into powdered sugar.

Tonight she was making candy, and the kitchen was filled with the good smells of melted chocolate, vanilla, cinnamon, dates, peanut butter, and coconut. Crist helped by cracking out all the English walnuts she needed, and Peter kept the woodbox filled with dry, split wood.

Dora made cherry bonbons and the traditional sand tarts sprinkled with red and green sugar. I did the cleaning up and dishwashing while they all traipsed outdoors to go sled riding in the moonlight. Nate and I walked out to watch them for a few minutes at bedtime. We were almost tempted to take a ride ourselves in the clear, cold air with the moonlight shimmering on the ice-crusted snow.

Peter and Crist used round dishpans. Martha, Dora, and Sadie all piled on the big toboggan. Tomorrow Rudy plans to hitch his horses to the big bobsled and take us all for a ride. Pam's going along, too. We'll sing Christmas carols, and then Pam wants us to stop at her house for cookies and hot chocolate. We don't often have such snowy sleighing roads, so we're really looking forward to it.

YEARS ONWARD

⠿

The Goal

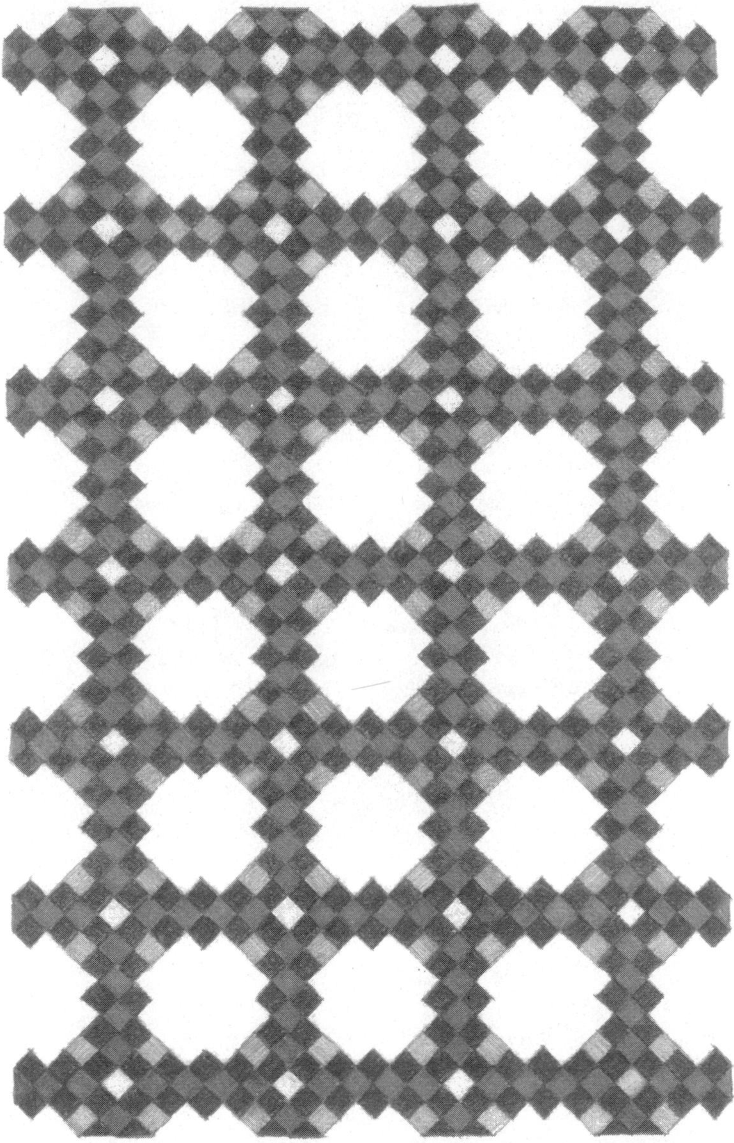

January 1, Year 17

A brand-new year. A time to think of new beginnings, making a fresh start in overcoming undesirable tendencies, and growing in grace and becoming more Christlike. Teacher Melvin had the scholars make a list of New Year's resolutions.

While cleaning Sadie's room, I found her list on her dresser. She had resolved:

1. Don't fight with my brothers.
2. Obey my mother promptly.
3. Don't daydream in church.

As for the first two, I wouldn't have thought it necessary for her to make those. She has a sweet personality, and I can't imagine her being disobedient or quarrelsome. She has inherited Nate's kindhearted nature, I believe, and I am truly thankful for that.

For Christmas, we exchanged names, and Peter drew mine. He gave me a hard-cover, two-year diary, and today I made my first entry. It's different from writing in my journal. There's a place to write daily, but only half a page is allowed for each day.

I have only a few pages left to fill in this journal. Now that I have a daily diary, I likely won't start another journal.

Keeping a diary takes the place of journal writing for me. I'll try to fill these last few pages, though, with some noteworthy thoughts and memories or even reporting on some special occasions. ▦

*W*ell, I guess this is noteworthy: Henry and Priscilla sent word that they have a nine-pound baby boy! His name is Raza Jethro. I wonder if Raza is an African name. It sure sounds *auslennerlisch* (foreign) to me.

They asked Martha and Chad to come and help them in their missionary work, and then to help them pack up and come home in about six months. Although Chad has enjoyed his stay here and his job, I think he was quite ready to see his homeland once again. Martha was eager to go, too.

Before they left yesterday, Martha told me that if she and Chad decide to get married, he will return with her. If not, he will stay in Africa. That is, if their plans don't change. I'm sure glad that they aren't making a hasty decision.

Priscilla wrote a long letter which I received today. She had a picture enclosed of little Raja with a curl on top of his head. He looks just like Miriam Joy did when she was a baby. Dora shed a few tears when she saw the picture. It doesn't seem fair that she won't get to hold him for so long. ▦

*O*h my, I see that several years have passed since my last entry. I don't like to leave things unfinished, so I'll see if I can fill these last few pages on this Sunday evening.

I was hunting for an old poem book and came across this forgotten journal. I have a good report to make of Dora. Our hearts are gladdened by the fact that this spring she intends to apply to take instruction classes and join the church.

Dora is giving her heart and life to Christ now at an early age. That is so much better than first sowing wild oats for a few years and waiting to join church until marriage plans are in the works, as some do. She is being a good example for Peter, Sadie, and Crist, who will be following in her footsteps in a few years.

I thank God for such a fine family, and that they are obedient and respectful. All too soon they will flee the nest, and then we will be left with the memories.

Henry and Priscilla returned from Africa and are back in their house. They have a ministry of taking care of babies whose mothers are in prison. Dora helps there several days a week.

Martha is in Africa, married to Chad, and they are both working as nurse's aides there in the clinic. Their plans to come back here never materialized.

As I had predicted, Pam's book is quite popular, if not a best-seller. But she is still in her humble trailer, the same good neighbor she always was.

Nate had another growth under his arm, which caused us some anxiety, but it proved to be benign again. Neighbor Eli was in a bad accident with runaways hitched to the corn binder. He was pinned between the binder and the barn wall and lay hovering between life and death for several weeks. But now he's on the road to recovery.

Life is a mixture of sunshine and shadows, sadness and happiness, failures and victories, trials and tribulations. Yet nothing can separate us from the love of God.

In Dora's book, *The Home Beautiful*, J. R. Miller says:

An artist painted life as a sea, wild, swept by storms, covered with wrecks. In the midst of this troubled scene, he painted a great rock rising out of the waves. In the rock, above the reach of the billows, was a cleft with herbage growing and flowers blooming, and in the midst of the herbage and the flowers, a dove was sitting quietly on her nest. It is a picture of the Christian's heritage of peace in tribulation. . . .

Thus Christ would have us live in the world—in the midst of the sorest trials and adversities, always victorious, always at peace. The secret of this victoriousness is faith—faith in the unchanging love of God, faith in the unfailing grace and help of Christ, faith in the immutable divine promises. If we but believe God and go forward ever resolute and unfaltering in duty, we shall always be more than conquerors.

What a picture of Christian living at its best! We strive for this goal, to have such peace even when sin threatens to overcome us and when "sorrows like sea billows roll" (Bliss). This is possible only when we are based on the rock that is Jesus Christ, who is both our sin bearer and our burden bearer.

With Paul, let us say, "Beloved, I do not consider that I have made [the goal] my own; but this one thing I will do: forgetting what lies behind and straining forward to what lies ahead, I press on toward the goal for the prize of the heavenly call of God in Christ Jesus." ✚

THE END
OF MIRIAM'S JOURNAL

Scripture References

YEAR THIRTEEN
Aug. 11: Job 1:21; Luke 2:51.
Sept. 6: Deut. 22:5; on the woman's cap, see 1 Cor. 11:1-16.
Oct. 29: Phil. 4:7; John 10:28-29; Matt. 21:22; John 15:7.
Nov. 12: John 2:1-11.
Nov. 13: 1 Cor. 3:11.
Thanksgiving Day: Ps. 136:1.
Dec. 10: Jer. 10:2-6.
Dec. 31: John 14:18.

YEAR FOURTEEN
Jan. 1: Ps. 59:16; Phil. 3:13-14; Ps. 103:12.
Jan. 24: Mark 13:32; Matt. 25:6.
Feb. 12: Rom. 8:6; 2 Cor. 12:9; Isa. 38:14.
Feb. 13: Eph. 6:4.

Mar. 15: 1 Tim. 2:1-2.
Apr. 24: Heb. 12:1.
June 2: Mark 10:16.
July 5: 1 Thess. 5:22.
Oct. 20: James 1:17.
Dec. 3: Mark 13:24-26.

YEAR FIFTEEN
July 25: Matt. 5:14-16.
Aug. 28: John 15:4.
Nov. 1: 1 Pet. 5:7.
Nov. 9: Matt. 16:26.

YEAR SIXTEEN
May 16: Acts 8:38; Luke 23:26.
May 20: Ps. 23:3; Rev. 21:4, 27; Job 1:21.

YEAR TWENTY
Mar. 20: Rom. 8:35-39; Phil. 3:13-14, NRSV.